I0772939

CYNTHIA HICKEY

Cowgirl Blaze

Cynthia Hickey

The Cowboys of Misty Hollow, Book 4

To all my fans who love cowboys!

Chapter One

Kentley Montgomery watched in horror as the roof of her house caved in, sparks flying in its wake. "Honey!" Her mastiff had gone back inside to save the teddy bear she wouldn't sleep without. Kentley had already lost so much to fire when she was little. She couldn't lose her dog.

"I got her." A fireman came around the corner, highlighted by the blazes behind him, with Honey in his arms. In the dog's mouth was the tattered teddy bear.

"Thank you. I owe you everything." She wrapped trembling arms around the dog after the man set her down and removed his helmet.

"Not a problem, ma'am." He smiled, the burn scars on his face pulling one side of his mouth into an awkward grin.

"Honey means everything to me." She gave the fireman an impulsive hug, then stepped back, keeping a restraining hand on her dog's head. "I'm in your debt." The nausea in her stomach settled.

Pleasure lit his dark eyes. "Just doing my job. Maybe we could have coffee together sometime."

Kentley's smile faded. "That would be nice, but I'm leaving town. I've got a job on a ranch in Arkansas. If you're ever in Misty Hollow, look me up." What had once looked like a friendly spark in his eyes now seemed darker, harder, and she took another step back regretting her invitation for him to look her up.

He gave a nod, turned, and marched to where the other firemen worked on putting out the inferno that had once been her rental home. Thank goodness, she'd packed her few things in the truck before retiring to bed. Since the house didn't have a garage or carport, her truck sat safely away from the fire.

"Wait, what's your name?" She called after the retreating hero who had saved her best friend.

"He's Ryan Moss," one of the other firemen said. "Man's not afraid of a fire, no matter how big the blaze. Got caught once when a beam fell. It's a wonder he survived. Now, he's the one who goes where no other firefighter will."

"Thank you. Is there any need for me to stick around?" Since there'd be no more sleep that night, she might as well start the drive to Misty Hollow.

"Nope. We've contacted the owner of the house. Since we have your phone number, we can call you if we have any questions." He left to join the others.

"Well, girl, let's go start our new chapter." When her stint as a bartender hadn't worked out, due to her recovering from liking the drink too much, she'd applied on a whim for the job as ranch hand. She'd grown up on a horse ranch, so the job seemed perfect for her.

She loaded Honey into the passenger seat of the truck, teddy bear beside her, then climbed into the driver's seat. With one last look at the place she'd called home for the last six months, she backed away and left Texas in the rearview mirror along with all the honky-tonks that had once lured her.

Good riddance, she whispered. All the bars' broken promises of helping her forget the childhood spent in one foster home after another. No one had wanted to adopt a frizzy red-haired, freckled-faced child who got into trouble more times than she could count. "That's all behind us now, isn't it, Honey?" She reached over and patted the dog. "A whole new life awaits us."

The dog's big, soulful eyes turned in her direction.

"I know I've failed you before, but I'm one-year sober. We're good this time. No worries, no troubles…just horses and cowboys." She laughed and turned her attention back to the road.

The sun hung high in the sky by the time Kentley pulled into the drive of The Rocking W. She let out a low whistle at the sight of the three-story, sprawling main house and the many outbuildings. "Looks successful, doesn't it, girl? Why don't you stay in the car while I introduce myself. Sometimes, you scare people." The dog's size often caused folks to take a step back until they realized she was as harmless as the stuffed bear next to her.

Her cowboy boots crunched gravel as she made her way to the front door. Before she could knock, a gray-haired woman wearing a frilly yellow apron opened the door. Kentley smiled. "I'm looking for Dylan Wyatt."

The woman smiled. "I'll go get him. Hold on for a

sec."

Kentley nodded and stepped to the edge of the porch to study the paddocks stretching down both sides of the drive. A smaller corral sat next to a large red barn. A long building looked like a bunkhouse. Behind that were several tiny houses.

"Ma'am?" A male voice.

She turned and grinned. "Kentley Montgomery reporting for duty." She thrust out her hand.

He frowned. "You're a woman."

"Yep, last I checked."

"I thought…from your name…"

"Happens a lot. I can do the job, sir." *Please don't send me away.* "I promise you."

"Well, you're here now." He glanced at her truck. "That a horse or a dog?"

Kentley laughed. "A dog."

He sighed. "We'll put you in one of the tiny houses. Go get your very large canine and follow me."

Kentley whistled, and Honey bounded from the truck's open window, teddy bear in her mouth. "Heel, Honey."

A smile teased at her boss's lips. "Let's hope the name fits. We've a few other new hands waiting out back to be shown around. We'll join them, then I'll leave you in the capable hands of Clay Jenkins."

She followed the man around the corner of the house where four men in boots and cowboy hats waited. Her boss introduced them as Clay Jenkins, Cody Hill, Levi Owens, and Trent Caldwell.

The one named Clay turned, his dark eyes widening at the sight of her. He removed his hat revealing hair the color of ripe wheat.

~

A woman? Clay frowned. Wearing a bright pink hat. What was Dylan thinking? Although, this Kentley Montgomery looked like a spring morning sunrise, a pretty woman would only cause trouble among the hands.

"Montgomery will stay in one of the houses," Dylan said. "Doesn't matter which one. This is her sidekick, Honey."

Clay dropped his gaze to the dog. Massive. "I hope she doesn't chase livestock."

"She doesn't." Kentley squared her shoulders. "I grew up on a horse ranch, most of the time anyway. Don't treat me any different than you would one of these men."

The other three men grinned like fools, reinforcing his fear that this woman would be trouble with a capital T. "Okay. Breakfast is at six, lunch is at noon, and supper is at five. If you're late, you'll go hungry. Follow me."

She had to hurry to keep up with his long strides.

"This is the barn, the bunkhouse you three men will be staying in. On the wall inside, you'll find the daily chore lists and the ones assigned to you. Montgomery, you'll stay in house number three. We'll get the key from Mrs. White, the cook. The boss is married to Dani and has twin sons, Eric and Derrick. Don't let the boys stop you from doing your jobs. They like to think they're helping." He glanced at his watch. "You'll meet them in fifteen minutes for lunch. Montgomery, if you want to pull your truck around, I'll meet you at your house with the key. Any questions?"

When none came, he ordered the men to stow their

things in the bunkhouse and entered the kitchen. Inside, he grabbed the key to number three off a hook near the door.

"So, the boss hired a woman." Mrs. White grinned. "About time."

"You're a woman."

"I came with the ranch when he bought it," she said with a laugh. "The boss didn't have a choice."

Clay chuckled and strode back outside as a battered Ford pickup pulled up to number three. He held out the key. "You'll start work in the morning, so you should have time to get settled in."

"Thanks." She took the key. "Don't worry. I can hold my own."

"I sure hope so." He pivoted and marched back to the house as the bell rang, signaling time to eat. "Leave the dog outside."

"Stay, Honey." The woman jogged to catch up to him. "Are you the foreman?"

"Nope. Maverick is, but he's away until tomorrow."

"What's he like?"

"A fair man. Married." He narrowed his eyes at her.

"I'm not here looking for a man."

He stopped. "Why not? Aren't most women?"

"I'm not most women." She planted fists on her thin hips. "Are you a chauvinist, Clay?"

"Of course not."

"Then don't say stupid things." She brushed past him, giving him a hard bump with her shoulder, and yanked open the kitchen door.

Despite Clay's reservations about having a female

ranch hand, he grinned. Montgomery might be fun to work with after all. She sure had spunk. He might as well go along for the ride. The woman might surprise him after all and do the same work as a man.

"So, what's your specialty?"

"Roping." She tossed over her shoulder. "I can hogtie and brand a calf in no time flat."

"We have mostly horses."

"I can break 'em."

"That I'd like to see." He grinned, picturing her on the back of a bucking bronco.

"Maybe you'll have the chance." She faced him. "The boss wouldn't have hired me if he didn't like my resume."

"He didn't know you were a woman."

"That shouldn't matter." Her hazel eyes flashed.

"Sometimes, the local sheriff deputizes us."

"So?"

"Sometimes, we volunteer to fight fires."

"Again, so what? I can do those things."

"If you two will stop squaring off like a couple of banty roosters, it's time to eat." Mrs. White glowered. "Act like the gentleman I know you are, Clay."

"Yes, ma'am." He gave a mock bow, waving Montgomery ahead of him.

Yep, this tall drink of a redhead was going to be fun.

Chapter Two

Kentley braided her hair into two braids that fell past her shoulders. She dared anyone to call her Pippy Longstocking—a nickname she'd abhorred in grade school. Then, slipping her feet into her worn cowboy boots, she grabbed her bright pink hat from a hook near the door and led Honey outside to do her morning business.

"This is a gorgeous place." Kentley rested her elbows on the tiny-house railing and stared at the woods behind the property. If she stretched and angled her neck just right, she could see a faint trail leading into the woods.

She glanced up, noticing a security camera. "I wonder why they need those way up here on the mountain."

Honey nosed around, clearly not caring about the cameras. When the cowbell rang out over the property signaling time for breakfast, Kentley led the dog to the back deck of the main house and told her to stay.

A large mixed-breed dog with gray around his nuzzle meandered over, introduced himself to Honey with a sniff, then the two lay down next to each other. "Honey's got a boyfriend," she sang.

"I told you women were always looking for a mate." Clay grinned from the bottom step.

"Ha ha." Kentley rolled her eyes and entered the house, letting the screen door slam shut before the man could follow.

"Rude." He stepped inside.

She smiled and headed for an empty chair at the table, eager to start her new job on a beautiful day. She hung her hat on a rack with the others, then sat and breathed deep of biscuits and thick white gravy.

"Eat up." Mrs. White handed her the plate of biscuits. "You need some meat on your bones."

Having a healthy metabolism, Kentley had always been on the thin side. "I'm looking forward to you trying to fatten me up."

"Kentley, we've got a mare in the far paddock that's resistant to training," Dylan said, ladling gravy onto his plate. "Your resume said you were good in that area. Care on making Smoky your first project?"

"I'd love to." Warmth filled her. "How old is she?"

"Three. Won't let anyone near her. She's beautiful and would make good breeding stock. You train her, and she's yours to ride." He grinned. "Until then, you can ride any horse in the barn, but make sure one of these ranch hands hasn't claimed the animal first."

The men started shouting out which horses they preferred.

Clay leaned close. "That leaves the doting ten-year-old Daisy for you. Sweet, but she plods along without a care in the world."

"Sounds perfect." Her heart fluttered as his breath

tickled her neck. She could tell the handsome cowboy was going to be a distraction. Nope. She refused to let him. A new life awaited her here on the ranch, one she intended to fully immerse herself in.

After breakfast, she went in search of Smoky. The cream-colored horse with a black mane, tail, and stockings snorted as Kentley approached.

Kentley perched on the paddock rail. "Hello, beautiful. You and I are going to be great friends."

The horse tossed her head.

"The boss wants me to train you, but I want to earn your trust first. What do you like? Sugar cubes or carrot sticks? I can bring both the next time I come and let you choose." Keeping her voice low, Kentley kept talking. As she rambled, the horse stopped her nervous movements and stared from a safe distance until Clay approached.

Kentley sighed. "I can't have folks coming up behind me if this is going to work."

"Sorry, but we're being called into town to help with a fire. Make haste, Carrottop."

She leaped from the railing. "Come, Honey."

Clay laughed. "I thought you were talking to me."

"Hardly." She rushed to where the other ranch hands had gathered. They all climbed into the back of a truck then Dylan sped away from the ranch.

"Won't the fire be too far gone for us to do any good?" Kentley glanced at the others. "We're not exactly close."

"Yep." Clay leaned against the cab. "The chief is working on putting us on the rotation at the firehouse, but he and Dylan haven't worked out a schedule yet. We're basically cleanup at this point."

They pulled up to a structure fully engulfed. Kentley shuddered, remembering how close she'd come to losing Honey just two nights ago. "Come, girl." She jumped from the bed of the truck and accepted the fireman's jacket handed to her. "Thanks." Without sparing the fireman another glance, she helped man a hose.

The same fireman who'd handed her gear, stepped up and helped her control the hose. "I've got this."

"Thank you, but I'm capable." She glanced at his shield. Something about his voice seemed familiar, but then the helmets muffled a lot of the sound that came through the radios. Stepping back, she looked to see where she could be of use. She couldn't tell the ranch hands from the regulars—only that there didn't seem to be many full-time firemen in the town of Misty Hollow.

She moved to the back of the building where flames scorched a dumpster. She grabbed a rusty bucket and tossed dirt on the flames. Once under control, she searched the area for other stray embers. Her gaze landed on a gas can and a book of matches without their cover.

Arson? She rushed back to find the fire chief and told him what she'd found.

"Good work, ma'am. We'll take it from here." He motioned to the fireman who had taken the hose from Kentley. "Check it out."

The man nodded and jogged to the back of the building, leaving Kentley feeling like an unneeded spectator. She removed her helmet and sat on the bed of the truck. The Misty Hollow fire department had gone from not enough fighters to too many.

She leaned back on her hands to watch as strong

streams of water put out the fire. The building would be a total loss, but from what she could see, it had been vacant.

The truck bed vibrated near her hand. She glanced down to see her cell phone. "Must have fallen out of my pocket." She glanced at the screen and frowned.

Good to see you again.

Again? Who in the world did she know in Misty Hollow other than those on the ranch?

~

"Good news." Clay hopped onto the truck bed next to Kentley. "We'll have a schedule at the firehouse by tonight." He narrowed his eyes. "What's wrong? You're staring at your phone as if you received bad news."

"Someone sent me a text saying it's good to see me again. I don't know anyone here." She glanced around, focusing on the crowd of spectators.

"Maybe someone you used to know moved here."

"Then why wouldn't they approach me and say hello? Something about this makes me antsy."

"Want me to notify the sheriff? That's him in the big hat." He pointed to a man in his forties standing next to the fire chief.

"No, I'm sure whoever it is will make themselves known. Maybe someone I was in a foster home with once."

"You were a foster kid?" He hadn't expected that bit of news.

"As far back as I can remember." She slid the phone into the back pocket of her jeans. "I met a lot of people that way."

"What was it like?"

She shrugged. "Mostly good, a little bad. No one wanted a kid like me."

"Like what?" His heart softened.

"A red-haired, freckle-faced troublemaker."

"I love your hair and freckles." Where in the world had that come from? He gave her a playful bump with his shoulder to keep things light. "As for being a troublemaker, we'll have to wait and see."

She laughed. "Hopefully, those days are behind me."

"A little bit of trouble makes a person interesting." He had a feeling Kentley Montgomery would be very interesting indeed.

She pulled out her phone and stared at the screen again. "I got another text. This one wants to know whether you're my boyfriend, or if I'm nice to every man I meet."

That held a hint of animosity in his opinion. "Why should it matter whether you're nice? I'm going to guess the answer is yes."

"I try to be." She studied the crowd again. "Maybe I should mention this to the sheriff."

"Stay here." He hopped down. "I'll get him."

"Sheriff, got a minute? I'd like you to meet Kentley Montgomery. She's received some texts that seem off to me."

The sheriff nodded. "Absolutely. I'm about to leave, but I have a few minutes. The chief suspects arson, thanks to Miss Montgomery finding the accelerant. I'd like to thank her for helping."

Clay hadn't known, but a ridiculous sense of pride swept over him that Kentley had spotted something the others had yet to look for. He led the sheriff to the truck. "Sheriff Westbrook, Kentley Montgomery."

The sheriff thrust out his hand. "Good eyes, ma'am."

"Thanks. I didn't have anything else to do, so I skirted the building. Anyone could've found what I did."

"Heard you've gotten a disturbing text?"

"Maybe." She told him what they said. "They don't seem very threatening, just…weird."

"They could be nothing. Don't erase them, though. Let me know if you receive any that are openly threatening."

"I will, thank you."

She and Clay scooted back as the other ranch hands returned to the truck. "I'm sorry again for disturbing you while you were talking to Smoky. Do you always spend time in conversation with a horse?" he asked.

She nodded. "When they don't trust people, I do. I need to earn her trust before attempting a bridle, saddle, or even laying my hand on her."

Made sense. "I think you're going to be a good asset to the ranch, Montgomery."

"Thanks."

The others congratulated her on finding the gas can as they piled into the back of the truck.

Clay smiled as her face turned a cute shade of pink. She obviously wasn't used to being praised. If she turned out to be good at her job, she'd better get used to it. The boss didn't hold back praise when due. The fact that she'd be the one riding Smoky if she was successful at training the horse said he believed in her.

The ride back up the mountain was filled with

Kentley being peppered with questions. She answered with a smile, clearly having nothing to hide until one of them mentioned a Saturday night drink at the bar.

"I'm a recovering alcoholic. Bars are off limits to me."

Perfection had a crack after all. Clay had met alcoholics before. The ones he knew fell off the wagon a few times. Would Kentley be one of them?

His father had been a raving drunk, who'd beat on Clay and his mother. He'd crashed his vehicle and died the night of Clay's high school graduation. The last thing Clay needed was another person like that in his life.

Chapter Three

A fist slammed into Kentley's jaw. *"I told you what would happen if the floors weren't done when I returned from town."*

Tears sprang to her eyes. "I'm sorry. It took longer to clean the barn than I thought."

"I don't want excuses!" Her foster mother loomed over her. "If you don't straighten up, I'm going to have you removed. Do you hear me? I took you in out of the goodness of my heart, and this is how you repay me?" Spittle flew from her lips as she raised her hand for another blow.

Kentley woke from the nightmare bathed in sweat. It had been a few months since she'd dreamed of the worst foster home—the last foster home before being moved to a group home.

Honey whined from the foot of the bed.

"It's okay, girl. I'm fine." She swiped damp hair away from her face and headed to the shower. The hot water washed away the remnants of the dream. Kentley was safe. No one woutld hurt her…beat her if she messed up on the job. The worst that could happen was getting fired. She kept repeating those things to herself as she headed to the door for breakfast.

Having forgotten her phone, she turned around and retrieved it from her nightstand. An alert told her she had another text. With her heart in her throat, she opened the screen.

Just checking in with you and hoping everything is all right. Your kindness to me the other day warmed my heart. I can't get you out of my mind.

The text seemed harmless enough, but Kentley's heart lodged in her throat. Who was this? Her fingers poised to respond but froze. She shouldn't encourage communication from someone she didn't know.

What if she did know them? No, they hadn't said that; they only mentioned her kindness. So, a stranger then.

She thought back over the last few days, but no one came to mind. Could it be one of the new ranch hands? If so, why not just come up and talk to her?

The breakfast bell rang, reminding her of the time. She'd worry about the texts later. For now, they didn't seem overly threatening. Maybe someone simply needed a friend. She'd have to think about whether or not to respond. What nagged at her though was how this person had gotten her phone number. She could count on one hand the number of people she'd given it to.

"Good morning." She took her seat at the table and stared at the mound of scrambled eggs and bacon. Mrs. White sure knew how to keep the ranch hands fed.

"Kentley, I'd like to speak to you after breakfast," Dylan said.

"Sure." Had she done something wrong already? It usually took her at least a month to need a talking-to, and that was usually the result of her sharp tongue. The food tasted like sawdust.

While the other hands talked about their duties for the day, she kept silent, trying to figure out why the boss wanted to talk to her. Maybe it was nothing more than her plans on working with Smoky. Yes, that had to be what he wanted to discuss.

She stood when Dylan excused himself and followed him from the dining room into his office.

"Close the door, please." He sat behind a large mahogany desk. "Have a seat."

She perched on a red and black plaid chair. "Am I in trouble?"

He smiled. "No, I simply have a question for you." His face settled into serious lines. "It's come to my attention that you may have a drinking problem."

"Not anymore." She squared her shoulders. "I've been sober for a year. It isn't something I try to hide. If you'd asked on my resume, I—"

"We're only clearing the air here, Kentley. Most of the hands have some sort of past." He folded his hands on the table. "I'd like to know what that past is, though."

She sighed. "I was also in foster care most of my life. I promise you my past will not affect my work here."

"I believe you. The ranch hands like to hit the bar sometimes on Saturday nights. They're going to ask you to join them. Will that be a problem?"

"No, sir. I can be around others while they're drinking." She'd drunk more than her share of sparkling water on such occasions.

"Good. Now about Stormy." He listened as she told him of how she preferred gaining the horse's trust before beginning training.

"It won't take all of my day. What else would you like me to do?"

"Whatever you see that needs doing. Mucking out the barn, cleaning the tackle…the ranch hands have tasks that are theirs alone, but the rest is whoever sees what needs doing." He settled back into his chair. "I trust my people know what to do. Tell me about the texts you've been receiving."

Okay, she knew who had run snitching to the boss. Clay was the only one who knew about the texts. "I'm sure they're nothing."

"This ranch has had its share of trouble, Kentley. If you feel at any time that you are in danger, I want you to let me know. We'll all stand behind you. You have a family here."

A family. Something she'd dreamed of her entire life and accepted that it would never happen. She got to her feet and blinked back tears. "Thank you, sir."

"Call me Dylan. Welcome home."

The tears fell as she left his office and headed for the paddock. People had been nice to her before, but no one had welcomed her into their family. Did she dare hope she'd found her place here on the ranch?

~

Ryan stared at his phone. Why wasn't she responding to his messages?

When he'd spotted a phone unattended in the back of the ranch truck, he'd opened it to find out who the owner was with the intention of returning it to them. Surprised to see it belonged to Kentley, he'd logged her phone number, seeing the perfect way to communicate with her.

Was it because of his hideous scars? He touched his face. They had repulsed others before her, but he'd seen the kindness in her eyes when they'd spoken. He'd believed her to be different than the others.

She was different. Kentley was special. The two of them could become great friends. She'd see. He'd get her attention and show her how much he cared—how wonderful they could be together.

~

Clay watched Kentley speak softly to Smoky, one hand stretched out, palm up. A carrot nestled there. The horse snorted and took a step back when she spotted him.

"I told you not to bother us." Kentley kept her voice low and didn't glance back.

"How did you know it was me?"

"I smelled your tattle-tale stench."

"Excuse me?" He sniffed his armpit. "I don't stink."

She jumped from the railing and stomped toward him. "You told the boss about my past drinking troubles." she poked her forefinger into his chest.

"I felt he should know." He clenched his jaw. "Some of the ranch work is dangerous. We all need our wits about us. The last thing we need is to babysit a drunk."

"I. Am. Not. A drunk!" She made a move to slap him.

He caught her wrist. "I still thought he should know. Look, we all have things that happened to us in our past. We've moved past them."

"So have I." She glanced at her dog who watched them, hackles raised. "It's okay, Honey. Clay is being a donkey's behind. I'm beginning to think he can't help himself." She turned back to Clay. "You also told him about the texts. Dylan is going to think I'm nothing but trouble."

"That isn't true." He told her of some of the trouble that had arrived on the ranch. "We know how to handle things."

"You're lumping me in with those things. Go away, Clay. I have work to do." She stormed toward the barn, her dog at her side.

Despite his reservations about her past drinking problem, he wanted to be her friend. He liked her spunk and the way she worked with Smoky. Clay sighed and followed her into the barn. "I'm sorry. I won't tell anyone your business again, not even the boss." Unless he thought not doing so would put someone in danger.

She grabbed a pitchfork. "Go away." She forked hay into a stall.

"Have you received any more texts?"

"None of your business." More hay flew.

"You have? Let me see." He held out his hand. "I want to help you, Montgomery."

"It wasn't threatening. Just someone thanking me for my kindness."

He frowned. "You don't know who? Have you responded to them?"

"No to both questions." She moved to the next stall. "Look, Clay. We work together, that's all. You don't have to try and befriend me."

"What if I want to be your friend?"

She widened those amazing eyes the color of a summer meadow. "Then you wouldn't have spilled my dirty laundry."

"Your past is nothing to be ashamed of. It's made you who you are."

"I'm not ashamed of my past." She returned to forking hay. "If I was, I wouldn't have said anything yesterday." She narrowed her eyes and leaned on the pitchfork. "Tell me about your past."

He gulped, not liking to talk about his childhood. "Things were rough when I was a kid."

"Rougher than mine?" She cocked her head. "The last foster mom I had beat me."

They were more alike than he thought. "My father was an alcoholic. Beat me and my mother. She lost several pregnancies because of those beatings. On the night of my high school graduation, he ran into some piling on the interstate. He died. Things were better after that. Then, a few years later, my mother died of cancer."

"I'm sorry." Tears welled in her eyes. "I can see why you reacted the way you did at my news."

"It's in the past."

"Same as mine." She wiped her hand on her jeans, then thrust it toward him. "Kindred spirits?"

He grinned and shook her hand. "Absolutely." Feeling better than he had in a long time, he saddled a horse and rode the perimeter of the property.

His thoughts kept returning to the fiery woman he'd left in the barn. Beautiful, hardworking, and wounded. If the texts she kept receiving became threatening, he'd do whatever he could to keep her safe.

A portion of the barbed-wire fence sagged, and he made a mental note to return later to make repairs. The few cattle the ranch raised for beef tended to strain against the wire to reach the grass on the other side despite the lushness of their enclosure.

Maybe he could convince Kentley to come back with him. He had some repair work to do between the two of them as well. Maybe he could request they be teamed up on the schedule at the firehouse. He'd make sure to put in a request.

He could keep an eye on her and any incoming texts, plus see whether he could move past the fact she suffered from the same affliction his father had. Would she turn back to drinking if the texts turned ominous? Could she handle the stress of working on a busy ranch and doing volunteer fire duties?

Only time would tell. He hoped to have what it took to help her if she'd let him.

Chapter Four

Kentley stared at the roster hanging on the wall of the bunkhouse. She had fire duty with Clay. Of course, she did. The powers that be seemed to thrust them together at every opportunity. Their first duty was that evening.

She shrugged and headed for the barn to see whether today was the day Stormy would allow a her to put on a lead. Usually, Kentley opened the door, and the horse rushed to the paddock. She hoped today would be different.

"Come here, gorgeous." She eyed Honey. "Why don't you move back. You might scare her."

The dog sat and stared up at her.

"Okay." Kentley chuckled. "Stormy should be used to both of us by now, right?" She grabbed some reins and opened the stable door. Keeping her voice low, she approached the horse who stomped and tossed her head.

"None of that now. You know I'm not going to hurt you. Shhh." She pulled a sugar cube from the pocket of her shirt and held out her hand. "Just a little closer, baby. Come on."

The horse nickered, then lipped the cube from

Kentley's hand.

Kentley lay a gentle hand on the horse's neck. When she didn't pull back, Kentley slowly slipped the bridle into place. The horse snorted. "Good girl. Let's take a walk, okay?" She carefully led the horse from the stable and outside to the paddock.

Rather than release Stormy, she kept talking and led the horse in a large circle, repeating the process several times until the horse followed as docile as Honey on her leash. Pride filled Kentley. What a wonderful horse she'd been tasked with. She couldn't wait to put a saddle on her.

"The boss told me he'd hired some new hands. I didn't know one of them was a woman."

Kentley stopped, noticing a cowboy she hadn't met leaning on the railing. "Hope that isn't a problem."

"Not from what I'm seeing." He grinned. "I'm Maverick Browning. Sorry I wasn't here to welcome you. The wife and I do search and rescue."

"Did you find who you were looking for?" She handed the reins to Honey. "Walk." The dog led the now docile mare around the paddock.

"We did. How did you know that would work?"

Kentley laughed. "I didn't until now." She thrust out her hand. "Kentley Montgomery."

He returned her shake. "Nice to meet you. Can you saddle break?"

"Yes. I'm hoping to do that next week. I believe in taking things slow."

"Well, it's working. I didn't think we'd ever break this one." He tapped his fingers against the brim of his hat and headed for the bunkhouse.

Kentley removed the bridle from the horse, fed her

a carrot stick, then headed to the chores awaiting her in the barn. She went to retrieve the shovel only to find it not where she'd left it. After several minutes, she found it lying behind a stack of feed. Strange. She would've never put it there. Kentley believed in always putting things back where they belonged.

Same thing when she went looking for the pitchfork, only this time she found it behind the barn lying in the dirt. She glanced around. Was someone playing tricks on her? Pranks on the new ranch hand? "Very funny, guys."

When she found the feed bucket in the hayloft, she stormed to the bunkhouse. Clay and one of the new hands, Levi—she thought his name was—glanced up from the papers they looked through.

"I've had enough. Who thinks it's funny to hide the tools I need?" Kentley propped her fists on her hips.

"What do you mean?" Clay frowned.

"Someone hid the shovel, pitchfork, and feed bucket. They weren't where I left them, and I wasted time looking for them."

"No one here would do that." He pushed to his feet. "Are you sure you didn't leave them out?"

"Positive. I know better than that. Maybe one of the new guys?" She narrowed her eyes at Levi.

He held up his hands. "Not me, and I haven't heard anyone say anything about hiding your tools. Usually, pranksters can't wait to get a laugh out of it from the other guys."

"Show me." Clay held the door open.

"I know what I'm talking about." Kentley marched to the barn. "See where the things are now?" She pointed to the tools leaning against the far wall. "That's where I always keep them."

"Okay." He moved around the barn. "I don't see anything else out of place."

"Nope. Just the things I use on a regular basis." Someone was definitely messing with her.

"I'll mention it to Maverick. He'll talk to the guys. If one of them is playing games, he'll stop them."

"Hmm." Clay would probably think she'd misplaced the things. "Thank you." She spun and headed for the house.

Her cell phone buzzed in her pocket. She slipped it free and glanced at the screen.

Did you sleep all right? I think of you every day.

Her heart skipped a beat and not in a good way. She replied. *Who is this?*

Don't you know? I thought we were friends. Your kindness took some of the chill from my heart that others had left behind.

She took a deep breath. *Sorry. I don't know this number.*

After several seconds of no reply, Kentley glanced back to the barn where Clay stood in the doorway. What if she shared the texts with him? She really didn't want to deal with this mystery alone. With a heavy exhale, she headed to him.

~

Clay took a moment to admire Kentley's long legs. Some of her unruly hair had escaped its braid and curled around her face. Worry lines creased her forehead. "What is it?" His gaze fell to her phone. "More texts?"

She nodded. "They aren't exactly threatening, but they're weird." She handed him her phone.

His blood chilled as he read the texts. Definitely more than weird. The underlying threat screamed Stalker.

"Do you think this person moved my tools?" Her eyes widened.

"It's far-fetched, but a possibility. There are cameras in the barn. Let's inform the boss in order to see the footage." He accompanied her to Dylan's office and showed him the text messages before explaining about the misplaced tools.

"Let's see." He booted up his laptop. "We definitely had a visitor." He turned the screen so they could see.

A man in a dark hoodie, being careful to keep his face away from the camera, moved tools around the barn. Why? What did such a stunt prove other than to torment Kentley? The man called himself a friend, so why do this?

Dylan's brow furrowed. "Since we have new hands now, we have enough to have a nightly rotation of perimeter checks. I'll have Maverick draw one up. Kentley, keep the door to your house locked at all times."

"Ya'll think this man is dangerous?" Her eyes darted from Dylan to Clay.

Clay nodded. "He might be. No sense in taking chances."

"Could this be someone from your past?" Dylan asked.

"I don't know who. I really don't know many people, and I never made close friends." She paled. "This sounds like someone I met recently, but I can't think of who."

"Think hard. I'm calling the sheriff." Dylan reached for his phone. "He'll need to know whatever you can tell him."

"Let's wait outside." With his hand on the small of Kentley's back, Clay led her to the sprawling front porch. "Have a seat. I'll get you a glass of sweet tea." Reluctant to leave her for long, he rushed to the kitchen, told Marilyn what he needed, and hurried back. "It'll be right out."

She gave a heavy exhale. "Clay, I don't understand. I haven't made any enemies."

"This doesn't sound like an enemy. It's probably someone you expressed kindness to, and they took it as a sign you had strong feelings for them."

"I try to be nice to everyone." Tears sprang to her eyes.

Marilyn brought out two tall glasses of sweet tea and oatmeal cookies. "Let me know if y'all need anything else."

"Thanks, we will." They sat without speaking until the sheriff's car pulled up, then both sprang to their feet.

He marched toward them and held out his hand for the phone. "You sure you couldn't tell who he was from the camera footage?"

"No." Kentley's hand trembled as she set down her glass. "He could be anyone."

He read the texts, then handed her back her phone. "I'll go take a look then come back to ask some questions."

"I thought coming to the Rocking W would be a fresh start after the rental I was in burned down." She returned to her seat. "After my childhood, being sober—"

"It is a fresh start." He reached over and took her hand, liking the way it fit perfectly in his. "We'll figure this out. Maverick told me how well you're doing with Stormy." Hopefully, talking about the horse would distract her a bit until the sheriff returned.

"She's a great horse. Very smart. I can't wait to ride her." She smiled. "She'll be a great asset to the ranch."

"Like the person training her?" He grinned.

"Better." Some of the stress left her face, returning when the sheriff joined them.

"You're right. Nothing distinguishing about the man," he said.

"Should I change my phone number?"

"No. Right now, he's only talking and playing silly games. The texts are our only contact with him. Just keep your return comments to a minimum. Above all, don't let him know he's rattling you. Forward all texts to me from this point forward."

"Okay."

They watched the sheriff return to his car and drive away.

"I am rattled, Clay." She faced him. "It'll be hard not to show it."

"It's easier not to show it when you text. So, what are you going to cook tonight? It's our turn at the station."

Her eyes widened. "I don't cook."

"Well, I guess I'll be cooking then. I make a mean chili. Let's head into town and pick up the supplies before it's time to check in. Meet me back here at three?"

"Sure." She collected their glasses and took them into the house.

Clay's smile faded. Someone had come onto the ranch. Someone with an obsession with Kentley. He'd have to keep a close eye on her. No one would harm her on his watch.

~

Ryan read the roster on the wall and scowled. His night off, and Kentley would be right here. This would've been the perfect time to get to know her better. He slapped the wall.

How had she reacted to his moving her things? It's what friends did to get a laugh, right? At least she'd had to have noticed.

He made the rounds of the other firemen, but no one wanted to change schedules with him. So be it. He'd find another way to get close to Kentley. It wouldn't be hard. Not with his skills. He'd draw her away from the firehouse, let her see him from a distance. See whether she recognized him or not.

It was too soon for them to talk face-to-face again. He needed to make sure that she didn't care about his scars. Too many gals pretended not to mind, then turned away when he made advances. How would he handle it if Kentley did the same? He touched his face. The scars were part of who he was. A hero, some people said. Who wouldn't want to be with a hero?

Chapter Five

Kentley listened intently as one of the full-time firemen, a David Miller, gave her a quick lesson on firefighting. This could be a disaster. She knew nothing about the subject.

"Have you ever fought a fire?" He frowned.

"No."

He turned to Clay and yelled across the room. "Hey, dude. What do you mean bringing along someone who has no experience?"

"None of us from the ranch had any formal training or experience when we started. We learned as we went." Clay glared from where he ladled chili into bowls.

"This is ridiculous. Hopefully, we won't have a fire tonight." He grabbed a bowl and plopped down at the table, grumbling to the other two full-timers.

"I'm sorry." Kentley accepted the bowl Clay handed her despite her appetite fleeing. "I'm just doing what I'm told."

"It'll be fine. You can handle a hose same as anyone, but like I said, we could use you to keep any spectators back." Clay flashed a grin. "Don't worry about them."

"Hard not to when they're sending daggers my way." She sat at the opposite end of the table from the three men and started to eat. The chili was good with just enough spice, yet not so much as to make her nose run.

After they ate, she washed the dishes while the men played cards, then curled up on the cracked leather sofa and channel surfed. When nothing caught her attention, she excused herself and went upstairs to bed.

The shrill ringing of the fire alarm jolted her upright a few hours later.

"Come on." Clay thundered downstairs.

Kentley followed and donned her gear before climbing into the fire truck, followed by Honey. A fire on her first night of rotation, and she had no idea what to do.

Clay patted her shoulder. "It'll be fine. Just follow Miller's orders."

She nodded, her heart in her throat.

The truck stopped on the edge of town where blazes quickly ate up what was left of an abandoned barn. Thank goodness no one had been inside.

She jumped from the truck, Honey right behind her, and glanced to where a handful of people stood watching. Crowd control. She could do this. Kentley marched toward them, back straight. "Stay back, folks. We don't want anyone getting hurt. Let the firemen do their job."

"Was it arson?" A man asked. "Had to be. We ain't had no lightning tonight."

"We don't know, sir; we just arrived." Her gaze fell on a man standing in the shadows of a massive magnolia tree. "Why don't you folks go stand by that man? He's at a safe distance."

When they did as she said, she joined the firemen next to the barn. "What do you want me to do?"

"Nothing." Miller cut a sideways glance at her. "Just stay out of the way. You shouldn't even be here." He turned on the hose, spraying it toward her.

She jumped back. "Not necessary." Refusing to be a liability, she made a slow perimeter check of the area. Behind the barn lay a book of matches—its cover torn off—and a gas can. Arson, same as before.

Movement in the trees to her left drew her attention. Someone moved through the shadows, but the clouds covering the moon made visibility difficult. That and the smoke rising from the burned embers of the barn.

Just in case someone was there, she waved and motioned them back to where the other spectators stood. The last thing they needed was for someone to get hurt.

"Montgomery? Get back here." The other fireman, Bruce Jones's, angry shout came through her earpiece. "We don't need you wandering off."

With an eye roll no one could see because of her helmet, she returned to the front of the barn. "It's definitely arson. Matches and gas can behind the structure." She crossed her arms. "I reckon that was something I could do with or without experience."

"Good job," Clay said.

"Anyone could've figured out the same, once they saw the evidence." Jones eyed Honey. "Get that dog and put him back in the truck."

"No one needs to because I've already done so." Kentley wanted to strangle the difficult man. "Would you like me to call the fire chief?"

"No, I don't want you doing anything. I'll call him." He turned off the nozzle and handed the hose to Clay before stomping toward the fire truck.

"A disagreeable man."

The last of the barn fell, sending sparks into the air like hundreds of orange fireflies. Honey whined and stared into the trees.

The sparks highlighted the figure of a man standing just inside the tree line. The arsonist? She tapped Clay's arm. "Look. It's the third time I've spotted him. The first time he was near the onlookers, the other two he was alone."

"Stay here. I'm going to confront him." Clay handed the hose to her. "Wind that back up, okay?" He strode toward the man.

Kentley returned to the truck and removed her helmet. Perspiration coated her hair to her face and neck. How did anyone wear all that gear without succumbing to heat stroke? She lifted her hair off her neck and raised her face to the slight breeze.

Honey's whine from behind the truck drew her. "What is it, girl…oh, no." She screamed, then covered her mouth.

Bruce Jones lay on the ground. The axe from the truck protruded from his chest. She backed away and peered around. Who did this? Were they still here?

Where was Clay or the the man he'd gone after? Neither was in sight.

A scream rose again. She stifled it. Her heart threatening to beat free, she called for Honey to follow and took off in the direction Clay had gone. No, she stopped in her tracks and spun around. Since she'd found the body, it was up to her to call the sheriff.

~

Jones had gotten what he deserved. How dare he speak to Kentley that way? She was only trying to do the right thing. The manshould've been glad for her help.

Hearing the cowboy thundering through the brush like a bull, Ryan continued toward where he'd left his truck. The man following would never catch him. He'd be gone within seconds of reaching his vehicle.

He grinned, the act pulling at the tight skin around his mouth. Kentley had probably already figured out the same person had set both fires. Wait until he revealed that he was that person? She'd have to be impressed. After all, fire was the best way to purge.

Soon, he and Kentley would be cleansed together.

~

The man was fast—Clay would give him that. The sound of an engine revving told him he'd lost the man.

An innocent person wouldn't have run. He had to be the arsonist.

He removed his helmet and carried it back to the scene of the fire in time to spot Sheriff Westbrook's car pulling up next to the fire truck. Clay quickened his pace to where Kentley waited. His eyes widened at the sight of Jones with an axe in his chest. "Had to be the person who set the fire."

Kentley explained about the matches and gas can. "Why would he kill one of the fire fighters, though?"

"Why set the fires in the first place?" The sheriff asked. "Thank God all the properties have been unoccupied buildings. Let's pray it stays that way." His gaze returned to the body. "One death is one too many.

We now have an arsonist who has committed murder."

"I tried to catch him, but he got away." A sense of failure almost choked Clay. If he'd just run faster, he would've prevented more fires and possible deaths.

"Thanks for trying." The sheriff sighed. "We'll get him; we always do." He turned as Deputy Hudson arrived with the crime-scene techs. "The fire chief is on vacation. Guess we'll have to handle this."

Clay and Kentley returned to the smoldering embers. "We'll stay until there's no threat of it reigniting or spreading, then head back to the station. You okay?" He tried to read her face.

"I'm fine. Why kill Jones, though?" She unzipped her jacket and pulled out her phone. "There's a new text. I'm afraid to read it."

"Let me." He took the phone. "*No one talks to my Kentley like that. Only kind words should be bestowed upon you, my dear.*"

"My stalker killed Jones?" Her eyes widened. "That means he is also the one setting the fires."

"Yes." The danger level had just increased for Kentley. "We have to let the sheriff know." Clay forwarded the message, but also returned to where the sheriff stood and handed him the phone.

He read it. "I don't want Kentley alone. At all. Not until we catch this guy."

"How did he know how Jones spoke to me?" Kentley asked. "He couldn't have heard unless he had a helmet with an earpiece."

Clay's heart dropped to his knees. "Every firefighter wears an earpiece. One of us?"

"Check to see whether any suits are missing. He could've taken one from the truck." The sheriff shook his head. "I can't believe it would be one of our firefighters. How protective is that dog, Kentley?"

"Honey will attack if I tell her to, or if she thinks I'm in danger. She's a teddy bear that can turn into a grizzly."

"Good. You might need that grizzly before this is through."

Clay could be dangerous, too, when the situation was warranted. He'd keep Kentley safe at all costs. Even if it meant his life.

It was a sober four who returned to the firehouse in the early morning hours. Without speaking, they all crashed on their beds.

Sleep was a long time coming for Clay. By the time he woke, the aroma of pancakes filled the place. When he padded into the kitchen, he noticed the two firemen who'd had the night off were sitting at the table. There was no sign of Kentley or her dog.

"Where's Kentley?" His heart lodged in his throat.

"We're out of coffee," one of them said. "The gal wanted some frozen-mocha thing. She was leaving as we arrived."

Clay did his best not to focus on the man's scarred face. "I'll fetch her from the coffee shop and head back to the ranch. Again, I'm sorry about your friend."

"We appreciate the sentiment." The man turned back to the stove.

Clay barged into the coffee shop as Kentley headed for the door. "Didn't you hear the sheriff tell you not to go anywhere alone?"

"I'm not alone. I have Honey." She wrapped those gorgeous lips around her straw almost making him forget how afraid he'd been to find her gone. No, he wouldn't be swayed.

"The sheriff meant for a human to be with you, Montgomery. You know that."

"I trust Honey more than any human." She brushed past him and out the door.

"Even me?" He asked, following her.

"You're quickly becoming a close second." A smile teased at her lips, then faded. "It's daylight, Clay, and the street is filled with people."

"One of whom could be the arsonist and murderer."

"Okay. I won't go anywhere without someone other than Honey."

"Good." Clay would start carrying his gun whenever he left the ranch with her. He wasn't taking any chances. "Did you get enough sleep last night?"

"No." She sighed. "I kept seeing Joneswith the axe in his chest. Knowing that the person stalking me did that…"

"Maybe you can take a nap this afternoon. I'm sure the boss won't mind." In fact, Clay would explain everything to him. Dylan might give Kentley the day off.

"I'll be fine. Working with Stormy is relaxing." She opened the passenger door on his truck, then glanced up and down the street. "I wonder if he's watching right now."

"Could be. Let's get inside so we can get out of here." His skin crawled at the thought that a murderer had his sights on Kentley.

Chapter Six

Kentley spent the next morning learning some basic firefighter skills. Clay had told her they would be doing this every day before their next rotation.

After hours of pulling hose lines, raising ladders, tying knots, breaking down doors, and covering rudimentary emergency medicine like CPR and treating minor burns, her entire body ached. "This is too much," she groused.

"Well, the next time the fire chief offers a day of training for anyone interested, I suggest you take it." Clay rolled the hose back on the fire truck. "It's nice of these guys to help you. Attending a more formal class will show them you appreciate their work."

"If they'd have waited until I had some training before putting me on the roster, Joneswould still be alive." Guilt burrowed deep into her gut.

"His murder was not your fault, Montgomery." A muscle ticked in his jaw. "Remember that. He was killed by a sicko obsessed with you."

Which still put her at the center of the trouble and the fireman's death. "I need to go back and work some more with Stormy."

"Okay. You've had quite the workout today." He

slung an arm around her shoulders as if they were pals. "And you'll repeat it all tomorrow."

"Yippee." She might've rethought the job if she'd known firefighting was part of her duties. Fire terrified her. Oh, sure, she acted brave enough, but the sight of flames sent sheer terror coursing through her.

Maybe she should say something. She glanced at the strong man beside her. No, he'd think her silly. After all, when they arrived at a fire, she wore the proper gear. There were others to do the dangerous work. She could do this.

"You okay?" Clay asked over the hood of his truck.

"Just tired." She climbed inside and clicked her seatbelt into place.

Levi approached her later that afternoon as she finished working with Stormy. "Hey, the guys are headed to Ray's, a local bar. We want you to join us."

"I don't do bars."

"There's nothing to worry about. No one will bother you with us there."

Oh, he must think she didn't want to go because someone would hit on her. "No, thanks."

"Come on. You're one of us now. Let's have some fun. You've earned it after all the hard work you've done. A couple of the guys already think you're standoffish."

Maybe because she was the only female ranch hand. She sighed. "Fine."

"Great. Meet out front at eight."

What she really wanted to do was go to bed early. Instead, she nodded and led Stormy back to the barn.

What could it hurt really? She had worked hard. It

would be good to get to know the men she worked with better. A person didn't have to drink liquor just because they went to a bar. She'd order water.

At eight, she joined the others in front of the main house, surprised to see Clay there. "You're going?"

He nodded. "I'm your bodyguard, remember?"

"I'm safe enough with these guys." She glanced around the group. What if she wasn't? What if one of them was her stalker? They were close enough to know what she did every day. Her phone number was in her employee file in the boss's office. Easy enough for one of them to get her number.

"Earth to Montgomery." Levi grinned. "You coming?"

"She's riding with me." Clay opened the door to his truck.

Levi shrugged and hopped into the truck with the others.

Once in the truck, Clay turned to her. "What's wrong? You don't have to go."

"It's not that." She folded her hands tight in her lap. "What if one of them is my stalker?"

His eyes widened, then he shook his head. "That won't happen. These men will step between you and harm. I know they will."

"Even the new hands?" She tilted her head, studying his face. "You don't know them very well yet."

"I know them well enough." He turned the key in the ignition and drove toward town.

Country music blasted her ears the instant she jumped out of the truck. Her heart raced and her palms sweated. Once, a place like this had been her downfall.

Was she really strong enough to step inside and not lose what she'd fought so hard to obtain?

She took a deep breath, squared her shoulders, and stepped inside the dim recesses of Ray's. Levi led the group to a far corner table and waved over a pretty blond woman. "Beers all around, sweetheart." He winked.

"Coming right up." She sashayed away.

"I think she likes you," Ryder said.

Kentley bet most women thought the ranch hand quite the catch with his ash blond hair and dark eyes. Not for her. He was too friendly and knew how attractive he was. She preferred the quieter Clay, even when he crossed the line into bossiness.

The server brought their drinks, setting a glass in front of each of them. Kentley stared at hers, then pushed it away. "I'll have water, thanks." She closed her eyes and exhaled slowly. First hurdle passed.

"You don't drink?" Cody reached for his bottle and poured it into the glass in front of him.

"No. I've been sober for a year." It felt good to say the words.

"I'm sorry." Levi's smile faded. "You should've said something."

"I'm okay."

"Tell us your story, Montgomery," he said.

"She doesn't have to tell you if she doesn't want to." Clay came to her aid. "Don't pester her."

"I don't mind." She smiled up at the server who brought her water. "My parents died in a fire when I was five. I barely got out alive, and spent the rest of my growing-up years bouncing from one foster home to another. The last home I was in…they beat me. I was then sent to a group home where one of the residents introduced me to liquor. For a while, it made everything easier."

~

Ryan stiffened. Sitting one table over with his back to the cowboys, he could easily hear the conversation that went on between songs. The band took their break at the right time for him to hear Kentley's story.

She simply needed cleansing. His gut had told him that the moment he returned her dog to her. It became more important than ever for him to take the necessary steps to bring her closer to him and to her final destiny.

Soon. With her training at the fire station, it became harder and harder for him to stay out of her sight. She'd recognize him the moment she saw him. Scars were hard to forget. But it wasn't time. Not yet. Almost.

Ryan tossed money on the table and, being careful to keep his face averted, he left the bar. He had plans to make.

~

Kentley stared at her phone. Clay noticed how her freckles stood out in stark contrast to her pale skin.

She bolted to her feet. "He was here. Close enough to hear my story." She whirled around, her hazel gaze roaming the room.

"Let me see." Clay took her phone. *It's good to know more about you, Kentley, but my heart broke hearing about how imperfect you are. Don't worry, my darling. Everything will be made right in time.*

"Who are we talking about?" Levi set his glass down hard on the table. "Is someone bothering Montgomery?"

Clay told the others about the texts and the stalker. "The sheriff doesn't want her going anywhere alone."

"This must be why the boss has us patrolling the ranch at night," Deacon said. "I didn't ask any questions."

"Don't worry." Ryder gave a quick nod. "No one will hurt Montgomery with us around. Do you think he's still here?"

"I don't know." Clay surveyed the room. No one seemed to be paying them much attention. The closest table sat empty. "Wasn't there a man sitting there when we arrived?"

The others shrugged. "I didn't notice," Levi said. "Maybe."

"Let's go." He gripped Kentley's arm. "It isn't safe away from the ranch."

"I'm surrounded by all of you. Whoever is sending the texts can't get close to me." She yanked free. "He's just trying to scare me."

It was more than that. He'd mentioned her being imperfect and how it would be made right. Things were escalating at an alarming rate. "Forward the text to the sheriff. Tell him where we were when you received it. I want him to know every detail."

She nodded and sat back down.

The mood around the table had grown somber. Not even Levi could be drawn into flirtation with the server.

Seeing how seriously the others took Kentley's situation released some of the pressure off Clay. They would look out for her. And, he hadn't seen one of them pull out his phone. Her stalker wasn't one of the ranch hands.

So, then who? It had to be someone close to her.

Someone who knew about her schedule. He drummed his fingers on the tabletop. She didn't go anywhere but the ranch and the fire station.

He frowned. One of the firemen? It made sense. But he'd known them for years. Except for the one with the scars. The man had seemed nice enough. Clay hadn't seen him talking to Kentley. What was he missing?

With the fun having disappeared from the evening, Levi suggested they head back. "Clay's right. We shouldn't have Montgomery out in the open."

Keeping Kentley in the center, the men formed a protective circle around her as they headed for the parking lot. Clay stopped, frozen to the spot. Two tires flat! He gritted his teeth as he approached the truck and examined each of them. The scoundrel had sliced them with a clean blade.

"Looks like we're riding back with all of you." He helped Kentley into the truck bed. He'd come back in the morning to retrieve his vehicle. Hopefully the bar had cameras for the parking lot.

Headlights followed them as they turned onto the road that led up the mountain. The vehicle continued to follow as they passed one turnoff after another. Unless someone was driving over the mountain to the other side, there wasn't much up there besides the ranch and a few hunting cabins.

Clay banged on the window behind him. "Levi, I think we're being followed."

"Not exactly a safe place for a car chase," the other man yelled out the window.

Clay agreed and wished he'd brought his gun. He'd left it on the ranch since Ray, the bar owner, didn't allow weapons inside his establishment.

"Maybe it's nothing," Kentley whispered.

"Maybe." They weren't the only ones who traveled the mountain road, but not many did at ten p.m. He gripped Kentley's hand. "We'll be home soon."

"I still can't figure out who would do this."

"I'm thinking one of the firemen."

She jerked around to face him. "Why?"

"You only go two places. The fire station and the ranch. I know it isn't one of the ranch hands. They didn't use their phones in the bar. That leaves the fire station."

"Clay." She clutched his arm. "When my rental house burned down, a fireman with severe burn scars saved Honey. I gave him a hug. He asked me out for coffee, but I said I was moving to Misty Hollow. I told him to look me up. Clay, I *invited* him here. I didn't mean it. I didn't think he'd actually come."

It had to be him. "This isn't your fault. There's a new fireman in Misty Hollow. He has burn scars."

Clay had been face-to-face with the man. They'd had a conversation. Kentley had been right there. His blood chilled. "We need to let the sheriff know." He reached for his phone.

The truck behind them increased its speed and passed by so close Clay feared he'd take the driver's side mirror off.

"Give me your phone." Clay pulled his out and called hers. "Tell me if you hear anything."

"I hear clicking."

"Is the recorder on?"

"I don't know."

Clay took her phone. A green dot showed at the

top of the screen. The man had been recording their conversations and tracking Kentley. That's how he'd known they would be at Ray's that night. "When was your phone out of your possession?"

"I left it in the truck bed the night we were at the firehouse. At the fire. It fell out of my pocket."

"That's when he must've put the tracker on." He turned and stared out the front window as rear taillights disappeared over the hill. The man had been a step ahead of them the whole time. Iff his suspicions were correct, he doubted the new fireman would show his face again any time soon, which meant the sheriff wouldn't know where to find him.

As soon as they pulled in front of the main house on the ranch, Clay jumped out and ground Kentley's phone under his boot.

Chapter Seven

Kentley tossed and turned that night, alternating between relief and anger that Clay had destroyed her phone. Was it a good thing or a bad one the man named Ryan Moss could no longer contact her? *If* he was the one tormenting her and setting the fires.

She stared at the ceiling. Of course, he was the one. How many scarred men had she hugged in her lifetime? Because of her a man was dead. Clay was wrong. It was her fault. She'd brought trouble to Misty Hollow. The best thing to do was to leave and take the trouble with her, but where would she go?

Reaching over to draw comfort from her dog, Kentley realized she wasn't in the bed with her. "Honey?" She peered over the loft to the floor below.

Honey stood, hackles raised, by the front door.

Kentley thundered down the stairs and peered out the peephole. Not seeing anyone, she slowly opened the door and stepped onto her postage stamp-sized porch. "What is it, girl?" She turned.

A sheet of paper tacked to the frame of the front window fluttered in the morning breeze. Kentley's hand trembled as she pulled it free. *"I know you. Now you will get to know me.*"

Her legs threatened to give way, and she sagged against the railing. He'd been here. Right on her front porch, and she hadn't known a thing.

How had he gotten so close? Who was on patrol? She ducked back inside, locked the door behind her, and quickly got dressed. She'd show Clay the note at breakfast. Kentley also needed a new phone, which she could order online even though it would take a few days to arrive. It wouldn't be difficult to request a new phone number.

Dressed, she rushed to the main house, frantically surveying the property as she ran. Honey loped at her side. Once they reached the safety of the back deck, Kentley told Honey to stay, then yanked open the back door.

Mrs. White whirled from the stove to face her. "Mercy, girl. You scared the dickens out of me." She narrowed her eyes. "You're as white as bleached flour. What happened?"

"I need to see Clay."

"He's in the front room with the sheriff."

"He's here already?"

"Bright and early."

Kentley hurried to join them and thrust the note at the sheriff. "This was on my porch this morning."

Sheriff Westbrook read the note, lines creasing his forehead. "Ryan Moss called the station early this morning and quit with no explanation." He folded the note and slipped it into his pocket. "It's hard to believe that a man hailed as a hero is capable of arson and murder, but he is our primary suspect as this time. Clay told me about your phone. I understand his thinking that the phone needed to be destroyed, but now that Moss can't contact you that way, he's going to get closer as he did with this warning note."

"What does do you think he meant by writing that I'll get to know him?" Kentley's heart raced.

"I can only speculate, but whatever I come up with doesn't bode well for you."

Clay moved to her side. "I'll stay close."

"No." Kentley narrowed her eyes. "That will only put you in danger."

"I can handle it."

"Well, I can't." Heat rose up her neck. "One person is already dead because of me." She held up a hand to stop his protests. "Say all you want, but Ryan Moss wouldn't be in Misty Hollow if I hadn't told him to come visit—look me up."

"It's more than that, Kentley." The sheriff put a hand on her shoulder. "We're dealing with a sick man who took your kindness as something more. An interest in him, maybe. Either way, you did nothing wrong. You expressed gratitude to him for saving your dog. That in no way warrants his actions."

She wanted to believe him. Her shoulders slumped. "If this doesn't turn me back to drink, I don't know what will."

"No." Sadness crossed Clay's face.

"I'm only joking." Sort of. "Don't worry. Even I know that drinking won't make the trouble go away." She padded to the back deck and stared into the trees, Clay trailing behind her.

At first, she'd thought of asking the boss to pull up the camera footage. Maybe he already had, but she knew what she'd see. A man in a hoodie leaving a note.

Ryan was too smart to show his face.

The other ranch hands trooped past her, all sending her curious looks. She wanted to shout at them for not doing their job, for letting danger get so close. What about the Wyatt twins? Would Ryan harm them to get to her? She didn't know how his twisted mind worked.

Fear rose up her throat, threatening to choke her. Her breath came in gasps.

"Sit. Put her head between your knees." Clay lowered her to a chair. "Honey, come."

The dog laid her large head on Kentley's lap.

"I'm okay." She forced the words from a tortured throat. "It's just an anxiety attack. I get them sometimes, but it's been a while."

"The events of the last few days would bring one on." He knelt in front of her. "What can I do?"

She covered her face with her hands. "Make it go away."

~

With every fiber of his being, he wished he could. "Don't worry, I'll help you through this. I promise I'll stick to your side like glue until Moss is behind bars."

"What if he comes at you like he did Jones?" She removed her hands, revealing red-rimmed eyes.

He forced a smile. "I think I can handle him. Jones wasn't expecting anything, but I'll keep my wits about me." He stood and pulled her to her feet. "Come eat. You need to keep up your strength. It's biscuits and chocolate gravy this morning with a mountain of bacon."

"Bacon and chocolate?"

"You don't know what you've been missing."

As if knowing Kentley needed him, the others had

left two empty chairs side by side. Clay pulled one out for her, then filled her plate with biscuits and butter, ladled on chocolate gravy, and placed five strips of bacon on the side.

"I can't eat all that." She shook her head.

"Then I will. If I don't put it on your plate, it'll be gone." He grinned. "These guys are piranhas."

"Sneaky." Levi waved a slice of bacon in his direction. "We've been filled in on the situation, Montgomery. Three men will be patrolling together instead of two. We'll catch this creep."

"Thank you," she said softly. "You don't know how much this means to know I have all of you with me."

"Hey, you're one of us. We're family." Levi shoved the bacon into his mouth. "No one messes with our family."

Kentley ate one biscuit and two slices of bacon, then slid her plate in Clay's direction. "I'll be outside working with Stormy. Before you say don't go anywhere alone, just know that Honey will be right there. She's the best warning system I can have. Besides, Ryan could've gotten to me by breaking into my place last night. Obviously, confronting me is not the plan right now." She stood and left the room before Clay could argue.

Without speaking, the others stopped eating whether they'd cleared their plates or not and went outside to do their chores. Clay knew without a doubt they'd find ways to work close to Kentley throughout the day. The pistols on their hips spoke volumes.

He sighed. The ranch had just become a modern OK Corral. "Sorry for all the leftovers, Mrs. White." He pushed aside his plate.

"No worries. It'll keep if someone gets hungry later." She started clearing the table with Marilyn's help.

"You know the trouble my daughter was in once," Marilyn said. "We made it through that, and we'll get through this."

"Yes, ma'am." Clay prayed the woman was right. He stepped outside. With a glance toward the paddock where Kentley leaned against the horse, letting the animal feel some of her weight, he went to the barn to fetch his own horse. Today was fence-mending day, and Ryder would be waiting for him since mending fences took more than one man.

As he rode the fence line, he discovered a section that had clearly been cut. The barbed wire lay tangled in the grass. Looked like he'd found where Moss entered the property. Shaking his head, Clay continued to where Ryder waited and let him know they had more than one section to repair.

"I saw some electrical wire in the storage barn," the other man said. "We could string it along until we run out. It won't hurt the cattle, but it might deter Moss a bit. If nothing else, it'll give him a jolt. Gives me a happy feeling just thinking about it." He grinned.

"Great idea. Let's let the man know he isn't the only one who can play games. I'll fetch it and be right back." He steered his horse to the storage barn.

By suppertime, they'd repaired the fence and strung the electrical wire, turning the voltage as high as was safe for the livestock. Clay's stomach grumbled, reminding him he'd worked through lunch, but a hole in the fence could've meant missing cattle or horses.

"I'll be ready to put a saddle on Stormy tomorrow." Kentley fell into step beside Clay on the way to supper.

"That's great? Once you've finished that, Maverick will most likely find another horse for you to break. You've shown a talent for such a thing."

"It's my favorite job." She smiled, the tension of the morning gone from her face.

"Have you ever been injured?"

"Oh, yeah. I've broken my arm, my wrist, and received more bruises than I can count. It comes with the job."

He hung his hat on a hook near the door and sat next to her at the table. "I don't like the idea of you with any broken bones."

She laughed. "Good thing you don't have a say."

He wanted a say in everything she did. Clay had to work at remembering they were both ranch hands. Not an easy feat when she looked so fetching with her hair frizzing around her face and her sparkling eyes laughing up at him. Yep, it sure was hard to think of her as one of the guys, especially with danger stalking her. What he wanted more than anything in the world at that moment was to fulfill her request to make it all go away.

What if he failed to keep her safe? Sure, Moss had only sent warning notes and texts, but that might end soon. One day, he'd come for her—make good on his promise of cleansing her.

Clay couldn't let that happen. Kentley had become important to him. He couldn't imagine a world without the feisty redhead in it. He'd do whatever it took, even if it meant drawing his weapon on another man.

Chapter Eight

Kentley woke bathed in sweat. She tossed aside the sheet and let the ceiling fan cool her and sweep away the remnants of her nightmare.

She'd been dealing with fire okay since arriving on the ranch, but having a firefighter stalk her after doing a rotation at the fire house—it all brought back the terror that the sight of flames sent through her.

She sat up and covered her face with her hands. How was she going to get through the job expected of her? Especially at the fire station? Her stomach roiled knowing tonight was another night for her to face her fear. Even with the training she'd received, she felt totally inadequate. What if she caved when someone needed her the most?

During breakfast, Clay sent her questioning glances although she did her best to keep up a conversation with the other ranch hands. Kentley needed to do better if she didn't want to answer a lot of probing questions. Fire scared her. It was as simple as that.

"Excuse me. Stormy is ready for a saddle." She stood.

"You're riding her today?" Clay asked.

"No, just getting her used to the weight of the saddle. I might stand in the stirrups, but I don't want to push her too much." She forced a smile and carried her dishes to the sink.

Stormy sensed Kentley's distress and balked at having a saddle put on her. After a tense half an hour, the saddle rested in place, the stirrups hanging loose. Kentley decided against cinching it or placing her weight in the stirrup. That would have to wait until she was in a better frame of mind.

Since the boss hadn't put a time limit on the horse's training, she intended to take things slow and easy. A horse who trusted the rider was a great gift, and she wanted Stormy to be the best horse on the ranch.

After the training, she brushed the horse down, fed her a carrot, and went to clean the stalls—same as she did every day. The mundane tasks helped take away some of the night's stress, and by the end of the day when it was time to head to the fire station, Kentley felt in a better frame of mind.

"You okay?" Clay faced her before turning off the truck's engine at the firehouse. "You've seemed out of it all day."

"Trying to work through all that is happening." She shoved her door open. "I'm fine. Really."

"Don't feel as if you have to do anything you aren't ready for." He turned off the truck and followed her into the building.

"The station is short two firemen, Clay." She frowned. "Ryan and the man he killed. If I don't step up and do my job—what is expected of me—then who will?"

"Me."

"You can't do it all." She shook her head and stormed to the kitchen. Since it was her turn to cook, she'd coerced Mrs. White to give her a simple, but delicious recipe. Supper wouldn't be served arguing with Clay.

"Why are you upset with me?" He followed and leaned against the counter.

"This is my problem, not yours."

Shock registered across his face. "This isn't something you should go through alone. Are you pushing me away?"

"If I have to." She slammed a pan onto the stove. "I'm making fancy grilled cheese. Leave me be, so I can work." Remorse at her sharp tongue filled her, even more so as hurt replaced the shock on his face.

"Okey doke." He marched from the room.

She placed both palms flat on the counter and fought to regain control of her emotions. Snipping at Clay would accomplish nothing. He was right. She couldn't do this alone, but having someone help her put them at great risk.

She slathered on brown mustard, then ham, spinach, and two kinds of cheese before grilling them. When she had a plate piled high with sandwiches, she grabbed two bags of chips from the cupboard and carried the lot to the dining table.

"This is the best I can do, guys. I'm not a chef." She set everything down and waited until Clay and the other two other firefighters had dug in. What was Misty Hollow going to do with an arsonist on the loose? She voiced her concern out loud.

"Langley is going to lend us a couple of their firemen." Seth Ransom took a bite of his sandwich.

"This is good, by the way. They should be here any minute."

"I need to make more sandwiches."

"No, they'll have already eaten. Sit. Relax."

A few minutes after minute, the alarm rang. Kentley bolted upright, her heart in her throat.

"It's a big one!" Clay slid down the pole. "Come on."

Not wanting to break a leg, she thundered down the stairs and grabbed her gear from the locker. She quickly donned the fire suit and climbed into the truck. Honey leaped in after her. "Where?"

"Apartment building." Clay fixed a hard look on her. "I know you're scared, Kentley. Do what you do best. Find the source of the fire if you can, and leave the fighting to us."

She nodded. "That I can do." She wrapped an arm around her dog's neck, drawing strength from Honey's presence. Kentley didn't know what she'd do without the steadying influence of her dog. She'd thought many times of having Honey certified as an emotional-support dog. Maybe it was time.

The fire had burned most of the first floor of a two-story apartment complex. People in nightclothes huddled together on the sidewalk.

"Did everyone get out?" Seth yelled.

"No. Frank Badger is still in there. Second floor, room 204." A woman clutched her housecoat around her. "He uses a wheelchair."

Kentley's legs threatened to give way. It was her parents' deaths all over again.

"Stay strong." Clay put his hands on her shoulders and gave her a shake. "Keep these folks back. I'm going to man the hose while Seth heads into the building."

She nodded, eyes wide behind her shield, and hurried toward the crowd. "Are you sure he's in there?" She asked the woman.

"He's always in there. Never goes anywhere." Tears streamed down the woman's face. "Smoke alarms started going off. The bottom floor burned hot. We all rushed out as fast as we could. By the time we remembered him—" She turned and buried her face into the chest of the man standing next to her.

Kentley turned her attention back to the blaze. What could she do?

~

Clay kept the hose trained on the door Seth had darted through. An inferno blazed inside the building. It was too hot not to have been intentionally set, at least according to those from inside. According to them, it hadn't been a slow burn, but a fast, ravaging one.

He glanced to where Kentley and her dog stood near the crowd. She'd be safe back there and at a far enough distance she wouldn't feel the heat. He needed to talk to Dylan about taking her off the rotation. She didn't belong there. Not with her fear of fire.

When Seth appeared with an old man in his arms, Clay breathed a sigh of relief...until Seth laid the man on a patch of grass under an oak tree. He glanced Clay's way and shook his head. The man hadn't made it out alive.

Clay waited to see whether Kentley would move around the building for the source of the blaze, but she stayed rooted on the sidewalk, one hand on her dog's head. He'd leave it up to the others to find out whether the fire was a result of Moss or something else.

By the time the fire chief arrived, the building was a total loss. The man muttered something under his breath and moved around the building. After a while, he returned. "Arson. Same as before. Matchbook and a gas can. Somebody find me Ryan Moss so I can string him up!"

"Mr. Badger is dead, isn't he?" Kentley moved to Clay's side.

"Yes. Whether smoke inhalation or the heat, we don't know." He reached out to put an arm around her, only for her to step away.

"Ryan killed another man."

"We don't know whether he died because of the fire."

"He did. I know he did." She whipped around and hurried to the fire engine. A few minutes later, she returned clutching a sheet of paper. "He's left a message. He was here, watching the entire time."

Clay took the note and read it out loud, "*My dear Kentley. Why are you standing off to the side and not helping fight the fire? This is all for you. The fire is preparing you for your cleansing. It's nothing to be afraid of. Fire is fierce, destructive, beautiful, and cleansing.*" Clay's gaze shot to hers.

"He plans on setting me on fire." She swayed as her knees buckled.

He jumped forward and caught her before she fell. "Medic!" He gently lowered her to the ground, stepping back as an EMT took his place beside her. Catching sight of the sheriff arriving on scene, Clay pulled himself away from Kentley to hand over the note. "The fires aren't going to stop."

"Doesn't look that way." Sheriff Westbrook sighed and peered at the smoldering remains of the apartment building. His gaze then fell on the body bag holding Mr. Badger. "I'll have the autopsy put at top priority, so we know whether or not Moss is responsible for another death. Is Kentley injured?"

"In shock, I think. She has a terrible fear of fire, and this latest threat was the final straw."

"Then, she's brave for even being here. I'll take the note. You go back to her."

"Thanks." Clay jogged back to where Kentley now sat up, an oxygen mask over her face.

"I'm fine." She removed the mask. "Just a moment of weakness. It won't happen again."

"No, it won't, because you aren't going back on rotation. I'm going to talk to the boss."

"It's part of my job. You told me that when I started on the ranch." She struggled to her feet.

"That was before." He narrowed his eyes. "There have been extenuating circumstances."

"Phooey. I promise this won't happen again. Don't you see that I need to be a part of bringing Ryan Moss to justice? I'll be watching for him next time, and you know there will be a next time."

"Absolutely not." He wouldn't be deterred. "He can get to you out here. The ranch is safer."

"I'm not going to hide while others die because of me." She poked her forefinger into his chest.

He barely felt it through the heavy coat, but the gesture hurt all the same. "Stop it." He gripped her upper arms. "You need to listen to reason, Kentley. I can't have him get to you. I can't."

Her eyes flashed. "How are you going to stop

him?"

"By keeping you close." He pulled her to him, wrapping his arms around her. She struggled for a moment, then stilled.

Was she finally giving in? No. She gave him a two-handed shove when he released her. "Do not manhandle me."

"Stop." He took a deep breath. "If Moss is watching, you may have just put a target on my back by fighting with me."

She froze, her mouth dropping open, then snapping shut. "I hadn't thought of that. I'm so sorry." Kentley leaned toward him and wrapped her arms around him. "Never would I willingly put you in danger. I...I don't know what's wrong with me. Guess I'm overwhelmed and taking it out on you."

"Shhh. I know. It's okay," He whispered, already feeling the bullseye growing between his shoulder blades.

Chapter Nine

With the addition of the firemen borrowed from Langley, everyone agreed Kentley was no longer needed on the roster. Last night was the first night she'd slept well in a week.

To make her morning even better, she sat in the saddle on Stormy's back. "Okay, gorgeous, let's take a little walk." She pressed gently with her heels against the horse and clicked her tongue.

After a toss of her head and little dance to the side, Stormy moved slowly around the paddock. After ten rounds, Kentley reined her to a stop and leaned forward, patting the horse's neck. "What a good girl."

She spotted Dylan heading her way and slid from the horse. The hard glint in his eyes clashed with the smile on his face.

"Good job with her, Kentley." He propped one foot on the bottom rail of the paddock. "You have a real gift."

"Thank you. What's wrong?" She removed the saddle and set it on the top rail.

"We got a phone call this morning." He pressed his lips together and exhaled out his nose. "From Ryan Moss. He's demanded that you go back on the rotation at the firehouse. Said he can't get you ready for your purging unless you work the fires."

Her blood chilled. "He admitted he's going to set more."

"Pretty much. I'm sorry, Kentley. But he's threatened to hurt the ranch or someone who works here if we don't comply."

She nodded. "Okay." She squared her shoulders. "I can do this." At least she hoped she had what it took.

"Sheriff Westbrook is putting an undercover deputy in the firehouse on loan from Langley. He'll be with you the entire time you're there."

"And Clay?"

He swallowed audibly. "Moss wants him there, too."

It was as she'd feared. Moss was also going after Clay. "I'll do whatever this creep wants to keep everyone safe."

"Don't do anything foolish." He fixed a stern gaze on her, then strode back to the house.

Define foolish. Kentley meant what she'd said. She'd do anything—even walk into a burning building if it meant no one else died because of her.

She led Stormy to the barn for her brushing. The soothing act did little to release the tension knotting between her shoulder blades.

Later that evening, she prepared potatoes for baking while Clay grilled steaks. They didn't speak, each lost in their thoughts. It was quite possible her behavior the day before had erected a solid brick wall between them that only something on the magnitude of an earthquake could bring down.

She sighed. It would be for the best if they kept a

respectable distance. Safer for Clay, even if it sent shards of glass through her heart. She'd always known romance and a family were not in her future. Not with the background she'd had. Not when stress could turn her back to her nemesis. If she didn't start drinking again after this whole mess with Ryan Moss, she'd consider herself free and clear from alcohol's demon hold. "Potatoes are ready." She set the tray of aluminum foil-wrapped potatoes near the grill.

"Thanks." Clay flashed a smile. "I've got this from here on. Go relax. You'll need your rest."

They both knew Ryan would set another fire. Why else did he want Kentley at the firehouse? She nodded and joined the other four firemen and fell onto the sofa.

David glanced away from the sitcom on the television. "Clay filled us in on why you're still coming. We're ready for whatever Moss dishes out. Don't worry, Montgomery. You won't have to get near the flames, and we're all watching your back."

The others nodded.

"Clay told you about my fear?"

"Sure, he did, although it wasn't hard to figure out seeing your reaction at the sites. You're good at finding the cause of the fires as well as the signs Moss leaves behind."

"Same signs he leaves at all his fires. Not hard." She sighed. Now, she really was a liability.

She dozed off, jerking awake when Clay brought in the steaks. Halfway through supper, the alarm went off. At least it wasn't dark this time.

Knowing the drill, she suited up and joined the others at the truck at almost the same time. She waved Honey into the truck, then climbed in after her.

David grinned. "It's nice having a station dog, even if it is only one night a week. Maybe we should get one full time."

She returned his smile, despite the ache in her stomach. "I'm sure the perfect one is waiting to be rescued from the shelter."

They spent the drive to a barn outside of town talking about dogs. When they arrived, a man rushed toward them. "I have livestock in there."

Those in the truck sprang into action. "Come, Honey." Kentley hated sending her dog into the inferno, but she would know what to do and would help herd the animals to safety.

Honey raced into the barn. A few seconds later, a horse darted out and thundered past them, then another. When the flames grew too hot, she put two fingers to her lips and let out a shrill whistle she hoped her dog could hear over the fire's roar.

Clay and one of the other firemen worked the hoses while the other two ushered animals from the barn. They exited when Honey did.

"Are they all out?" Kentley asked, motioning for Honey to sit next to her.

"We think so. The barn will be a total loss—same as the other buildings." He removed his helmet and splashed water from a nearby trough onto his face and over his head. "Good dog you have." He replaced his helmet and went to help keep the fire from spreading to the house.

"You are a good dog, aren't you, girl?" She patted Honey's head. "And since your teddy isn't here, we didn't have to rescue you this time." Kentley would make sure to leave the dog's toy at home when it was her turn at the station.

She scanned the area. *Where are you, Ryan?* She had no doubt the man watched from somewhere close. He wouldn't want to miss the show. She went to circle the barn and find the book of matches.

A man stood in the shadow of the main house. When she caught sight of him, he crooked his finger, beckoning her to him.

~

Clay jumped back as the barn roof collapsed sending sparks into the late afternoon sky. He glanced to where he'd last seen Kentley. She was gone.

He yanked off his helmet to let the afternoon breeze cool his perspiration. "Anyone see Kentley?"

"She was just there with her dog," one of the men shouted.

Clay swallowed past the boulder that had lodged in his throat and dropped the hose. Where would she have gone?

He headed around the smoldering pile of what had once been a barn. Kentley was walking toward a man near the main house. "Kentley!"

She stopped and turned.

The man dashed into the trees.

"What are you doing?" Clay gripped her arm. "Are you crazy?"

"I wanted to confront him. Ask him to stop before someone else dies." She yanked free. "It was the only way to make this all stop."

"His final plan is to kill you."

"Maybe I can talk him out of it." Her gaze searched his. "He's obsessed with me. If I go to him— let him think I feel the same way he does—then he might stop."

"What if he doesn't?" Fear as cold as an iceberg filled him.

"Then it will still be over."

He shook his head. "I thought you were smarter than that. Too smart to put yourself in harm's way."

"I know what it's going to take to stop him." She brushed past him. "We can't fight about this. I'm sure he's still watching."

Which meant Moss would think Clay a danger to the woman he obsessed over. "Fine, but this discussion is not over." He'd bring it back up in the privacy of the ranch. Clay fell into step beside her. "You mean too much to me, Kentley. We're in this together."

"It's my problem."

"Not anymore. It's the problem of me and the rest of Misty Hollow. People are dying."

"I know that," she hissed. "That's why I need to stop him."

"We'll find another way."

"Come up with a better idea, and I'll gladly listen." When they reached the truck, she peeled off her suit. "I don't have a death wish, Clay."

"Could've fooled me," he muttered.

She shot him a look that should have left him in a pile of ashes. Instead of saying anything else, she pressed her lips into a thin line.

Let her be angry with him. Under no circumstances would he let her face Moss alone. Not even with her dog. The mastiff would do her best to protect Kentley, but the dog was no match for a bullet if Moss pulled a gun. Not that Clay thought he would shoot Kentley. No, the man seemed very clear that he intended to burn her in a fire—maybe leave her scarred as Moss was. No doubt, the man would join her in the flames.

By the time they left the crime scene, night had fallen. Kentley went to bed without speaking to him again. He sat on the sofa and flipped through the television channels, stopping on the local news which reported on the fire.

The reporter went on to say that the police had the identity of the arsonist but refused to disclose the suspect's name. She finished by saying the public had the right to know.

Maybe they did. Or at least a photo of the man. Someone might see him around town. If the authorities wouldn't disclose Moss's identity, maybe Clay should. The sooner the man was behind bars, the better.

~

Ryan sat in his truck by the lake just outside the campgrounds. He couldn't rent a motel room or book a site at the camp. The police would be on him in a second.

He drummed his fingers on the steering wheel, already tired of living in his vehicle. What he needed was to find a place to hole up. He contemplated a hunting cabin on the mountain, but decided the police would suspect that, too.

What was going on with Kentley and the cowboy? One minute they were in each other's arms; the next they were spitting like two rival cats. He couldn't tell whether the man was a threat to Kentley or not.

Maybe he should get rid of Jenkins. He needed Kentley's undivided attention, and the cowboy was a definite distraction for her. The problem would be getting close to the man. Everyone knew of Ryan's plans for Kentley. They'd be on guard. She'd never be alone. Tonight would've been perfect if Jenkins hadn't come along looking for her.

Ryan needed a better plan—one that would bring Kentley right to him.

Another problem was the massive dog she took with her everywhere. The beast would be too smart to be lured away from her owner. He'd have to dispose of the dog as part of Kentley's cleansing. There wouldn't be another way.

He'd known the moment she'd given him a hug that they were meant to be together for eternity. The only way for that to happen was for him to bring her into the fire with him.

It wasn't time. He leaned his seat back as far as it would go and closed his eyes. No, it was definitely not time yet. Kentley needed to be a hero first, and he had to be the one to make that happen.

Chapter Ten

Clay tossed and turned all night, reliving the argument with Kentley. He knew without a doubt that she'd confront Moss at the first opportunity. Alone, most likely. Again, the urge to release his identity welled. The people of Misty Hollow deserved to know.

His phone buzzed from his nightstand. In his haste to grab it before it woke up one of the other ranch hands, he knocked it to the floor.

With a groan, he snatched it and glanced at the screen.

Careful, Cowboy. Hurt Kentley and suffer the consequences. She has not fulfilled her fate yet. I will make her a hero that will not be forgotten. Soon.

Clay's blood ran cold. Moss couldn't contact Kentley anymore, so he'd turned to him. His hand shook as he set the phone back on the table and grabbed a clean pair of jeans from the drawer.

It didn't take a genius to know that making her a hero probably meant her death. For it to be of the magnitude that no one would forget, it would involve other people. People who would die.

Dressed, he rushed to the main house to wake Dylan. His boss answered the knock on his bedroom door in baggy shorts.

"It's early, Clay." He rubbed his face.

"This is important. Can you step outside?" No need to wake his wife.

"All right." Dylan grabbed a shirt from the back of a chair and pulled the door closed behind him. "I get the feeling this is bad."

"Yes, sir." When they reached the back deck, Clay showed him the text message. "The people who mean the most to Kentley are here on the ranch."

"And Moss has already struck once."

"As a warning, I think."

Dylan's features formed into hard lines. "I'll notify the sheriff and figure out where to send my family." He lifted his gaze to Clay's. "We've weathered storms before, so we can handle this one, too. Have the men gather in the barn after breakfast. I want them all to be aware of the potential danger. Kentley, too."

"She's already insisting on facing Moss alone."

"We can't let that happen. I'll talk to her. The sheriff will, too." With a nod, he handed back Clay's phone and entered the house, leaving Clay to face his fears alone, at least for the moment.

His gaze drifted to the tiny house Kentley lived in. She would need to move to the main house for her safety. Living out there alone, security cameras or not, left her in a dangerous position.

She'd balk, saying that staying in the main house put everyone else in danger. True, but they were all in this together now. The barn fire made sure of that.

A few minutes later, Kentley stepped onto her front porch, a cup of coffee in her hand and her dog by her side. Seeing him, she waved and smiled.

He waved back and stepped off the deck to head her way. The look on his face caused her smile to fade.

"What is it?"

"I got a text from Moss." He handed her his phone.

"He's going to burn me." Her eyes widened.

He frowned. "What?"

"When I first met him at my house fire, someone told me he got his scars by being a hero. He's going to make me a hero the same way." She sagged against the porch railing. "My worst fear is going to come true."

He took the cup of coffee from her hand before she spilled it and set it on the railing before pulling her into his embrace. "I won't let that happen. I promise."

"You can't keep that promise if you're dead." Her words were muffled by his chest. She raised her head. "He'll go after you and the others before he comes for me."

"Dylan is letting everyone know. We'll all face this threat together."

She shook her head. Tears streamed down her face. "I need to do this alone."

"No." He tightened his hold. "I won't let you. If you leave, I'll follow you. Your leaving will put me in danger. Do you want that?" He wasn't above using guilt to convince her to stay.

"No, but you're already in danger."

"Safety in numbers." He forced a smile. "Come on. Let me and the others fight this with you. You're part of a family now, Kentley. Remember that."

"I don't know how to act in a family."

"Let me teach you." He planted a tender kiss on her forehead. "Let's have breakfast. The boss wants all of us in the barn afterward to let us in on his plan. I'm pretty sure Sheriff Westbrook will be there."

She sighed. "All I want is for this to be over. I'm so sorry you're in involved in this. I should've left after the first text."

"You had no idea what Moss had planned." He took her hand, holding it tight as if she'd bolt and run. "I'm glad you're here."

"Then, you're a strange man."

"Yep." He opened the kitchen door and waved her inside. He wasn't so strange. The red-haired, freckle-faced woman in front of him had found a place in his heart and was burrowing in. He liked the feeling and wasn't ready to let it go. To let her go.

Kentley ate her pancakes in silence, only speaking when directly spoken to. Clay let everyone know the boss wanted to hold a meeting after breakfast and glanced at Dylan's empty seat. Dani and the boys had also stayed away. Had they already left the ranch?

Kentley glanced at the empty chairs at the table several times and sighed. No doubt she blamed herself. He wished he could make her see that none of this was her fault, but that of a madman's.

~

Kentley joined the others in the barn and waited for their boss and the sheriff to join them. She perched on a bale of hay, fear rippling through her despite her attempt to stay strong. Be a hero? Hardly. She wouldn't be able to face a fire with bravery. Kentley straightened as Dylan and the sheriff entered the barn, both looking as if they were carved in stone.

"The text, Clay." Sheriff Westbrook held out his hand for the phone. Deep lines formed on his forehead as he read. When he finished, he returned the phone.

"Forward that to me and any others you receive. There's no point in you buying a new phone. Moss will still find a way to contact either you or Kentley."

Dylan told the others what the text said, holding up his hand when shouts of outrage filled the air. "I've sent my wife, sons, and mother-in-law on a vacation until this is over. Mrs. White will be leaving within the hour to spend time with her sister in Oklahoma. We'll all be fending for ourselves until Moss is behind bars, taking turns with the cooking and cleaning." He turned his attention to Kentley. "I don't want to hear another word about you thinking you can face Moss alone. He brought the fight to my ranch when he burned down my barn. Got it? We're facing him as a solid front."

She nodded and swallowed past the lump in her throat. She really was part of something greater than herself—surrounded by people who cared about her. Kentley could only pray none of them would be harmed because of her presence.

"I want to hear the words from your lips," Dylan said.

"I promise not to search for Moss on my own."

"Or leave the ranch."

She exhaled heavily. "Or leave the ranch without telling someone where I'm going."

"No leaving the ranch without me." Clay took her hand.

"Okay." *God, help me keep my promises.* Even as she prayed, she knew she'd break them in a heartbeat if it meant saving Clay or one of the others.

"We'll keep our rotation at the firehouse because the town depends on our volunteers." Dylan crossed his arms. "Sorry, guys, but we also have to step up patrol of the ranch. We're all going to be stretched thin for a while."

"We got this," Levi said.

"Absolutely," River added. "This ain't our first rodeo."

Dylan grinned. "I don't know any better folks to face this kind of threat than those in this barn right now. I appreciate all of you. Keep your eyes open and your wits about you." With a nod, he left the barn.

"That's that." Kentley stood. "Thank you, all of you, for your support in this. But, please don't take any unnecessary risks."

"We'll do what needs to be done." Clay gave her hand a squeeze. "Now, go fetch that pretty little pink cowboy hat and give Stormy a ride. She'll cheer you up."

She gave a small laugh. "You're right. Care to join me? Let's see how she does out of the corral with another horse alongside."

His smile faded. "Can you handle her if she doesn't like it?"

"Of course, I can. Otherwise, I wouldn't suggest it. Stormy will be fine." Excitement welled at the thought of taking the horse for a genuine ride.

Horses saddled, she led Stormy from the barn, whispering encouraging words as the mare tossed her head and snorted at Clay's horse. "Shhh, beautiful. It's just a handsome guy."

"I hope you're talking about me." Clay grinned over his horse's saddle.

"Of course." She laughed, swinging into the saddle on Stormy's back. "Come, Honey."

With her dog following, she headed the horse past

the buildings and into the open. Other than a little sideways dance, Stormy settled down and seemed to enjoy the ride. Kentley leaned forward and patted her neck. "You're a marvel, sweet girl."

"You've done a great job with her." Clay pulled alongside them.

"It's not difficult when you have something wonderful to work with." Oh, how she wished Stormy belonged to her. On her salary, she couldn't afford such a magnificent animal. "I'm glad Dylan said I can use her while I work on the ranch."

"Few things better than a good horse. Follow me. There's a great creek a short way ahead, then we can turn back. It'll be a good first ride for the mare."

Kentley fell back, glad to let Clay take the lead and curious to see how her horse would handle another being in front. After a disapproving snort, Stormy settled down.

Clay led them into the dimness of the woods. The dirt muffled the sound of the hooves as birds serenaded or scolded from the branches overhead. The late morning sun flittered through and cast rays of gold on the trail.

Soon, the babbling of a creek over rocks reached her ears. Honey raced ahead of them.

"This is one of my favorite spots." Clay slid from his horse, leaving it to graze on a patch of grass.

Not quite trusting Stormy not to run off, Kentley looped the reins over a low-hanging branch before approaching the creek, its water clear enough to see the pebbles at the bottom. She stuck her hand in. "Ice cold."

"Runs down from the mountain." Clay handed her

a protein bar. "It's clean enough to drink if you're thirsty."

"I can see why you like this place." She unwrapped the bar and took a bite of granola and dark chocolate. "Stay, Honey."

The dog turned from where she had started to go back the way they'd come. She turned and stared down the path, hackles raised.

"Clay?" Kentley softly drew his attention to her dog. "We aren't alone."

He pulled a pistol from his saddlebag. "Get behind me."

"I can shoot." She retrieved her own handgun and moved as quietly as possible back the way they'd come, leaving the horses behind. "Stay with me, Honey."

Right where the trail left the woods and the open expanse of the ranch stretched in front of them, a sheet of paper fluttered from where it had been tacked to a tree. With a trembling hand, Kentley reached for it, an icy fist gripping her heart.

I'm always watching. I'm always near.

Chapter Eleven

Kentley paused in the doorway of the fire station. Everything in her wanted to turn and run, but Ryan had made it very clear that she was to be there when scheduled, or someone would pay. So, here she was praying there wouldn't be a fire but knowing there would be. It's what Ryan did.

"I'm right behind you." Clay's assurance urged her inside.

David Miller stirred something on the stove, barely giving them a glance. "Stew is almost ready."

"Thanks, man." With his hand on the small of her back, Clay led Kentley to the table. "I'm always right here. Remember that."

She nodded, biting her bottom lip to keep the tears at bay. What had she done to deserve such a friend? Was he more than a friend? She studied his strong back as he headed for the stove. He was becoming much more than a friend to her. Did he feel the same? Dare she hope he did? Or were her feelings simply the result of the circumstances thrust at them?

No. Now was not the time to dwell on romance. She needed all her focus to stay alive and keep those around her out of danger.

Realizing Clay intended to serve her, she pushed to her feet and grabbed a bowl. "I'm not an invalid."

"I know that." He grinned. "I'm also pretty sure you didn't sleep very well last night. Not after the note we found."

True, but she didn't need to be babied. "Thanks, but I've got this." She held out her bowl to David who filled it, still not meeting her gaze. "Everything okay?" she asked.

"Sure. Why wouldn't it be?" He ladled a healthy serving into Clay's bowl.

"You seem to be somewhere else." She forced a smile she didn't feel.

"A bit of a headache. It'll pass."

"Is it just us three tonight?"

"Yep." He turned off the stove. "Rick is on vacation until Monday."

The already-stretched crew was stretched further. Again, she hoped for the impossible—t hat there would be no fire that night. She wouldn't be able to hang back with only three of them.

Her hand trembled as she brought a spoonful of stew to her lips. She'd have to fight the blaze right alongside the two men.

As if sensing her distress, Honey leaned against her leg. Kentley patted the dog's head, knowing Clay wasn't the only one to stay by her side. Honey never left her. She didn't know what she'd do without either one of them.

That night, as she started to drift into sleep, the alarm went off. Heart pounding in her throat, she quickly donned her firefighting gear and joined the men in the truck. "Where is it this time?"

"The strip mall on third." Worry creased Clay's face. "Not an empty building. Every space has a small business operating out of it. The fire seems to be contained to the flea market next to the café."

A brick building. Hopefully, the damage to the stores would be minimal.

The blaze did seem contained to the one section. Smoke billowed into the night sky, blending gray with inky black.

Kentley grabbed a hose and approached the blaze, then turned the nozzle to full force. The hose bucked in her hands. She planted her feet and held on as Clay did the same beside her. Where was David?

"Miller, where are you?" She spoke into her headset.

"The alley. I've found the source of the fire."

"Go on," Clay said. "I've got this. You're good at spotting the arsonist's tricks."

She turned off her hose and motioned for Honey to follow her. The only light in the alley came from the fire. Kentley pulled her flashlight from her jacket and clicked it on. She squatted next to the tell-tale splatter of accelerant and the book of matches. Of course, Ryan had set the fire. What did he want from her this time? She glanced around for David and called out his name.

A groan came from behind the dumpster. She rushed in that direction. When she rounded the block wall that hid the dumpster from view, someone hit her in the back of the head. She crumbled to the ground to the sound of Honey's growls.

Not fully unconscious but not exactly coherent, she could do nothing as David gripped her ankles and pulled her toward the fire. "I'm sorry, Kentley. He'll kill my family if I don't do this."

She tried in vain to let him know they were there to help him and his family—that the sheriff would provide protection, but her lips wouldn't move. The words stuck in her throat.

Honey's growls faded. Clay asked whether everything was okay. "Miller's headset is off. Kentley?"

Would he come to save her before it was too late? Was Moss watching to see whether David followed orders?

Darkness consumed her.

~

Ryan grinned as he watched through the binoculars. Miller had followed his orders to a T. Kentley wouldn't be out for long, then she'd feel compelled to save the fireman. This was her first test. The next fire would be bigger, stronger—preparation for her finale.

As Miller and Kentley disappeared into the flames, Ryan lowered his binoculars. She wouldn't die. It wasn't her time. The dog would alert the cowboy, and all would be well. This time Ryan climbed down the fire escape across the alley and approached the burning building. He could make out two forms inside, one standing, the other on the floor. Flames billowed around them. *Come on, Cowboy. I'm counting on you.*

If he didn't come around the corner soon, Ryan would have to act fast to keep Kentley from burning prematurely. He glanced to where he expected the man to show. When he spotted him, Ryan whipped around and darted in the opposite direction.

~

"Hey, stop!" Clay gave chase until he caught sight of Kentley and Miller in the fire through the window. He raced inside and gripped Kentley under the arms, dragging her free. He raced back inside. "What's going on, Miller?"

Miller stood there, the flames licking at his suit. "I had to. He was going to hurt my family."

Clay grabbed his arms and shook him. "Come on, before we both die. No harm, no foul, right? Kentley is fine." He hoped.

"My wife will be ashamed."

"She'll be grateful for your sacrifice." He tugged on the other man. "Don't make me die in here. You save lives, not take them."

His words spurred Miller into action. He shoved Clay from the fire and followed. Miller removed his helmet. "You're right. I don't want to die like that. Not at the whim of a madman."

"Great. Now call an ambulance for Kentley, and put out that fire." Clay rushed back to where he'd left Kentley.

She'd removed her helmet and sat slouched against the wall in front of the dumpster. "Moss made him."

"He told me. Are you all right?"

"Yes. Don't tell anyone, Clay. I don't want him to get in trouble. He had a good reason for what he did."

"There should still be consequences."

She shook her head. "Not this time. You and I would've done the same thing."

Probably. "Miller is calling for an ambulance."

"I don't need one. That will raise questions." She struggled to her feet.

"It's too late." Sirens wailed in the distance. "For

the ambulance and this store."

"Things can be replaced." Her eyes widened. "I almost died in that fire." Her legs gave out, and he caught her.

"I don't think that was the plan. Moss was watching you. He'd have pulled you out in time."

"How can you be so sure?"

"Because he has something bigger planned for you." He led her to the front of the building, handed her over to the paramedics, and turned his hose back onto the flames. Later, when they returned to the firehouse, he'd dwell on how close he came to losing Kentley.

Clay felt certain Moss would've saved her tonight. He got the impression the man wanted to be 'cleansed' right alongside her. So, why involve Miller? To show they couldn't trust anyone? Anyone could be bought for the right price.

Where would the grand finale take place? How could Moss take her if Clay never left Kentley's side?

He glanced over his shoulder to where she sat in the ambulance. As long as Clay had a job to do, something to keep him away from her, there would be opportunities. Like tonight.

Perspiration ran down his spine. He couldn't keep her safe. Clay was an idiot for thinking he could. Moss would come for her, and Clay wouldn't be able to stop him.

The man already called all the shots by ordering Kentley to serve her time at the fire station. What other demands would he make? What hoops would he make her jump through? What would he ask of Clay?

Flames extinguished, he turned off the hose at the same time Miller did. "I guess you heard through your headset that Kentley wants this kept quiet."

"I did, and I disagree. I'm going to come clean with the sheriff. She could've died tonight, and it would've been my fault." He put the hose he'd used back in the truck. "Keeping quiet isn't her decision to make."

Clay agreed, but he could understand Kentley's reasoning. "You've got to do what you think is right. However, you realize arson and attempted murder are felonies?"

"Yep." His shoulders slumped. "See ya."

Another fireman lost. Clay had no doubt the man would spend years behind bars. At this rate, the only ones left to fight fires in Misty Hollow would be the ranch hands of the Rocking W and the men they could borrow from Langley. The ranch hands wouldn't be enough to stop Moss. That left it up to Clay and Kentley.

"I'm good," Kentley said, stopping at his side. "What's going on in that head of yours?"

"Miller is going to the sheriff. He feels like he should. That means it's going to be up to you and me to stop Moss."

She frowned. "What do you have in mind?"

"I don't know yet." He'd come up with something.

"I'll think about it, too. We need to lure him into a trap."

Clay agreed, and the thought scared the dickens out of him. Things could go very, very wrong.

"Kentley." Sheriff Westbrook marched toward them. "Miller told me what he did on orders of Moss."

"I'm not pressing charges, sheriff." She crossed her arms. "I'm fine, the fire is out, and the man felt as if he had no choice."

"It will be considered attempted murder." The sheriff matched her stance.

"He feared for his family."

"Doesn't matter. I don't make the law, Kentley. He's going away for a long time."

Clay smiled at her tenacity, knowing she ran on adrenaline right now, but later, when she calmed down, the terror of being in the flames would consume her. He'd make sure he was there to comfort her. "Can we head back?"

Without speaking, a white-faced Miller climbed into the back of the squad car, leaving Clay, Kentley, and Honey to return to the firehouse without him.

Clay helped a trembling Kentley out of her gear and ushered her to bed. "I'll be right there. Wrap up in a blanket. I'll bring you something hot to drink." He cupped her face. "I'll stay with you until the fear is gone."

"It might never leave."

Then he would stay with her forever.

Chapter Twelve

The alarm at the firehouse went off again as dawn broke over the mountain. Kentley broke out into a sweat at the thought of fighting another fire so soon after her latest run-in with the flames. She wasn't as convinced as Clay that Ryan would've pulled her out before it was too late.

"Where is it this time?" She asked, thundering down the stairs while Clay slid down the pole.

"Apartment complex." Clay shot her a worried glance. "Fully rented."

God, help them. Calling for Honey, she raced for the truck.

By now, Honey knew the drill and darted around the building, nose to the ground, leading Kentley to where the fire had started in a corner apartment. Smoke alarms wailed from other apartments in the building as residents pushed and shoved to escape the billowing smoke.

"Is everyone out?" She asked, joining Clay as he fought the fire with a stream of water.

"The people say yes."

"Same MO out back. It's Ryan."

"I had no doubt. Here." He handed her the hose.

"I'll get another one. Duvall is checking to make sure everyone got out."

She nodded, praying no one had died that morning. Shortly after their return, two firemen arrived from Langley to replace the firemen shortage plaguing Misty Hollow.

Rather than let her fear of fire consume her, Kentley focused on the fact she still walked and breathed. At least only one apartment had caught fire, and everyone seemed to have gotten out.

She glanced over as one of the borrowed firemen, Keith Duvall, exited the building, a pet carrier in his hand. He held it up for her to see.

"Puppies." He set the carrier at her feet. "The momma is hiding under the bed. I'll be right back."

"Be careful." Her heart lodged in her throat as Clay motioned for him to stay, and he would go in his place. Why did he feel the need to be a hero? How could she fight Ryan if something happened to Clay?

She kept her gaze locked on the apartment entrance until Clay returned, the momma dog in his arms. Soon, the canine family was reunited. "Don't do that again." Kentley glared at him.

"It's my job."

"Keith was willing."

"He'd already been in there long enough."

"I need you." Her words broke off on a sob.

"The fire is contained, sweetheart. The smoke can't get into my helmet. I was perfectly safe." He clapped her on the shoulder and took the hose. "See to the dogs."

"Distracting me won't make me less upset with you." She carried the pet carrier to the waiting ambulance. "I know you aren't vets, but I think the momma could use some oxygen."

The paramedic smiled. "We can do that."

Kentley turned as the sheriff arrived. "Moss again?"

"No doubt," he said.

"Clay and I want to make plans to lay a trap."

The sheriff narrowed his eyes. "That's too dangerous."

"No more so than what's been happening. I'd rather confront him on my own terms rather than have him surprise me." She removed her helmet and lifted her face to a refreshing breeze. "Eventually, someone else is going to die. Maybe we can prevent that."

"The next person might be you."

"Then so be it." She refused to be dissuaded. "Either you help us, or we'll go it alone." By us, she meant her. She wouldn't involve Clay without the protection of the local sheriff's department.

"I've called in the FBI. Let's see what they have to say."

"When will they arrive?"

"Later today. Why not meet us at the office at three this afternoon."

"Okay. I'll give you until tomorrow, then I move ahead with whatever I can come up with."

"Are you giving me orders, Miss Montgomery?" He arched a brow.

Not answering, she simply smiled and rejoined Clay. She told him about the FBI arriving and her conversation with the sheriff.

Clay laughed, turning off the hose. The corner of the apartment complex was now a stark black against the morning sun. "The sheriff will try to stop us."

"He can try. I'm going to stand firm on this. It has to stop."

"I agree, but we'll have to be careful. The FBI might surprise us and agree to help. They have more experience than we can ever hope to have."

True, but she didn't hold onto the idea that they would agree to use Kentley as bait. She'd listen to their ideas but doubted anything else would work. Ryan wanted her. The rest was merely a game to him.

With her mind set on action, some of the fear she'd carried on her shoulders the last few weeks slid off. Hot anger had replaced the chill fingers of fear. She would confront Ryan and put a stop to his insanity. Somehow, she would win this fight.

~

After catching a few hours of sleep, Clay waited on the front porch for Kentley. The sheriff had texted that the FBI had arrived and were filled in on the latest details of the case. Now, it was time for him and Kentley to present their plan. Unfortunately, other than setting some kind of a trap, they didn't have a plan.

"I'm ready." Dark circles under Kentley's eyes showed the lack of sleep over the last few days. "Stand firm with me, Clay."

"Always." He put a hand on the small of her back, relishing the warmth emanating through her shirt. Someday, he wanted a normal day with her. A time of picnics and restaurants, horseback rides and fishing. Simple pleasures to get to know her better, so he could let her know of his growing affection for her.

Now was not the time. A romance formed under the threat of danger couldn't be trusted, could it? Was their shared love of ranching enough? Until now, he'd never thought past the next day, happy to be where he was. If he were to fall in love, would the woman be content as the wife of a ranch hand, or would she want something more? Maybe Clay could pursue a career as a fireman. Would Kentley be okay with that considering her fear?

Idiot. Why was he dwelling on something that couldn't happen? Not now, anyway. He'd defer thinking on such things until Moss was out of the picture.

They were each lost in their thoughts on the drive into town. A black SUV sat parked in front of the sheriff's office shouting to the city that the FBI had arrived.

When Clay and Kentley entered the conference room, Sheriff Westbrook introduced Special Agents Snowe and Larson. "They're familiar with Misty Hollow."

"Unfortunately," Snowe said. "We've been here quite a bit over the last couple of years. The sheriff has told us about Ryan Moss, but we'd like to hear it from you, Miss Montgomery."

Clay took a seat next to Kentley while she told them of meeting Moss when her rental house caught fire, after the man had saved her dog. How strange that someone so heroic could turn into someone so evil. A man who had once saved lives now took them.

"We dug into Moss's background," Larson said. "Until recently, the man had an exemplary record. Something triggered him."

"Me." Kentley hitched up her chin. "A simple act of kindness from me."

The agent nodded. "Because of that, this man is now obsessed with you. He believes the two of you belong together. As severely scarred as he is, I'm sure some people turn away from him in disgust. You didn't."

"No, I hugged him." She folded her hands in her lap hard enough to turn her knuckles white. Her knee bobbed under the table.

Clay reached over and placed his hand over hers to still her.

She shot him a smile of gratitude before turning back to the agents. "We want to set a trap for Ryan."

The agents shared a look of surprise before Snowe spoke again. "You would be putting yourself in grave danger, Miss Montgomery."

"If you put a wire on me, then you can move in and take him."

"I agree with Kentley," Clay said. "This has to stop. If we don't do this as a group, I'm afraid she'll go off on her own, and none of us can save her then."

"That's right." Kentley pulled her hand free from his and crossed her arms. "One way or another, with or without your help, I'm doing this."

"We can put you in protective custody, ma'am." Larson folded his hands on the table.

"Then you'd have to put me under twenty-four-hour surveillance." She matched his posture. "I know this might be foolish. It probably is, but it's something I need to do. I started this, and it's up to me to finish it."

"Us," Clay injected. "You aren't doing this alone."

Kentley stood. "I told Sheriff Westbrook I would give you until tomorrow to decide on our course of action." The rest of her meaning was clear. She'd go it alone if they didn't help her.

Clay stood. "I guess we'll be seeing you in the morning." He ushered Kentley from the room before the agents could say anything else.

Outside, he grinned. "You've got guts."

"About time I grew a backbone."

"You've always had one, darlin'. You just needed a little prodding. How about supper at the diner? Have you been to Lucy's?"

"No."

"Then you're in for a treat. It's within walking distance." He led her down the street to the diner where they sat in a corner booth near the window.

A waitress handed them menus and told them of the night's special of pork chops, mashed potatoes, green beans, and a roll. "I'll be right back to take your order. What can I bring you to drink?"

"Diet soda for me." Kentley turned to her menu.

"Coffee, please." Clay left his menu unopened, intending to order the special. "What's your plan if the FBI refuses to help?"

"Since Ryan texts you now, I'll send him a message on your phone to meet me somewhere."

"And then what?" They needed every detail worked out if this was going to work.

"He'll make a move and I'll counteract." She shrugged. "I don't really know, to be honest."

"That isn't good enough."

She gave a heavy exhale. "I know. That's why I'm really hoping the agents will help. If not, I'll go with Ryan and find a way to escape while leading the authorities to him."

Clay slapped the table. "This isn't the movies,

Kentley. Things aren't that simple. Every detail needs to be worked out. You can't act on the spur of the moment. That will get you killed."

She flinched. "I'm working on it."

"We need to work on it together." He gritted his teeth and turned to look out the window in an attempt to gain control of his emotions. Yes, he'd agreed to help her so she wouldn't go at this alone, but thinking of what could happen to her filled him with dread.

"I'll be okay, Clay." She reached for his hand.

He drew back. "You don't know that."

She sighed. "I do. For the first time since this all began, I'm filled with peace."

"That's anger talking."

"Maybe, but it's better than debilitating fear." She tilted her head. "We'll figure out what to do, and it will work."

"It had better." Because he didn't want to live without her.

Chapter Thirteen

Honey's growls woke Kentley. It took a moment for her to realize the dog's distress. When she did, she bolted from the bed and to the window. Flames ate at the tiny house she'd stayed in just days ago.

"Fire!" She slid her feet into slippers and thundered down the stairs, her dog on her heels.

A sleepy Dylan darted from his room and chased after her. "Wake up the hands." He quickly passed her and burst open the back door.

Kentley switched directions and headed for the bunkhouse. "Fire!" She banged on the door. "All hands on deck."

After a shirtless Clay yanked open the door, Kentley made a beeline for the water hose. The tiny house would be a total loss, but they could prevent the fire from spreading to the main house and other buildings. Hopefully.

How had the fire started? Could Ryan have gotten onto the ranch despite all their precautions?

"Here, let me. You train water on the barn." Clay jerked his head toward the nearly repaired barn after the last fire. "Try and keep the sparks from settling."

She nodded and changed direction again until she

heard one of Honey's rare barks. Disregarding the barn, she sprinted back toward the burning house.

Honey nosed around the back of the building. Ryan had tossed the tell-tale can of gasoline and a book of matches to the side. A brown box sat close to the flames.

Kentley snatched it up. Her heart seized at the sound of a kitten's plaintive meow coming from inside. The monster had put an animal's life in danger. If Honey hadn't alerted her, the box would've caught fire. She opened the box and tucked the frightened kitten down the front of the tee-shirt she'd slept in, then she dashed to douse the barn. Anger rolled through her as hot as the flames eating the tiny house and most of her belongings.

Fire had taken so much from her over the years. She wanted it to stop.

Ryan had to know she'd moved into the big house, right? So, what message was he trying to leave by burning the tiny house and endangering a kitten?

By the time the fire truck and sheriff arrived, the fire was out, and the house sat in a pile of smoldering rubble.

"Is your shirt meowing?" Clay arched a brow.

"I found it in a box behind the house. It was definitely Ryan." She freed the tiny black and white kitten and held it up. "It's a boy. I'm going to call him Blaze."

He stared at her as if she'd lost her mind. "How can you be so calm? Moss came within feet of where you slept."

"I'd like to know how he did that."

"You and me both." Dylan crossed his arms. "Who

was on duty within the last hour tonight?"

"Lincoln and Willy," Clay said. "Let me fetch them." He hurried away.

Dylan eyed the kitten in Kentley's arms. "A gift from Moss?"

"Yep." She sighed and knelt to let Honey sniff the bundle of fur, then straightened when the sheriff joined them. She repeated her account about finding the accelerant and kitten.

Clay returned with the two men who had been on patrol.

"I swear, Boss," Willy said. "We were doing our job. The man is like a ghost."

"Maybe there's a clue as to how he did it on the video feed," Lincoln replied. "We made the rounds multiple times."

The rest of the hands gathered around. Protests and words of outrage and revenge filled the air.

Sheriff Westbrook held up his hands to quiet everyone. "We'll find out how this happened. Right now, you need to keep your heads on straight. We don't need any vigilantes running around town." He shot a quick glance at Clay and Kentley. "The FBI are here and formatting a plan. The two of you are still planning on coming by the office later, correct?"

"Yes," they said in unison.

Kentley wanted to know what the agents had planned. Plus, she needed to buy supplies for the kitten. Thankfully, Dylan hadn't said she couldn't keep the dear thing.

"Let's take a look at the security footage." Dylan led her, Clay, and the sheriff to his office and pulled up the footage from an hour ago.

Kentley peered over her boss's shoulder as a figure dressed all in black slunk along the back of the buildings, staying to the shadows. "You can hardly tell he's there."

"Which is how he was able to set the fire." Dylan stiffened. "We need motion-activated lights everywhere. I don't want this man anywhere near my ranch or my hands again. If I see him, I'll shoot first and ask questions later."

"Hold on, Wyatt." The sheriff glared. "You can't take the law in your own hands."

"I'm protecting what's mine. If you don't like it, then catch this guy!" He lunged to his feet. "I sent my family away because of him."

Kentley stepped back as tensions rose.

Clay took her hand. "They're just letting off steam. It's okay."

"Someone is going to throw a punch," she whispered, her gaze focused on the two red-faced men. She'd never seen either of them lose control of their emotions before.

Dylan stepped within inches of the sheriff. "This man is costing me money and sleep."

"You aren't the only one who wants him caught. I've got a whole town to protect." The sheriff matched his stance. "We will catch him, Dylan. You know we will. Has my office ever failed yet?"

Dylan's shoulders relaxed. "No."

"That's right. So, instead of getting your hackles up, let's work together to stop Moss."

Clay's phone rang. He frowned and answered. "Clay Jenkins."

"Let me speak to Kentley."

"Moss?"

"Let me speak to Kentley."

Clay handed her the phone. "He wants to speak to you."

Her hand trembled as she took the phone. "Yes?"

"Good job on saving the kitten. You've passed your first heroic test of saving a life."

"If not for my dog, the poor thing would've died." She clutched the phone hard enough for her hand to ache. "Leave the innocent out of this."

"In order for you to be all that you can be—forgive the military cliché—the innocent has to be involved. The tests will get harder, but I trust you're capable."

She took a deep breath. "Why don't you stop and just meet with me?"

"In due time." He hung up.

She returned the phone to Clay. "I passed the first test."

~

"What test?" Clay slid the phone back into his pocket.

"Saving the kitten. Are we done here? I'd like to go back to bed for another hour or so." She glanced around the room.

When the sheriff nodded, she slipped from the room, taking the cat and her dog with her.

"Is she all right?" Sheriff Westbrook asked.

"She's too calm, if you ask me." Clay tore his gaze away from the door. "She's gone from being terrified of the sight of flames; now she's actively wanting to confront a madman. It worries me. What does the FBI have planned?"

"A town meeting at nine. Make sure you and

Kentley are there." The sheriff marched from the room.

"I shouldn't have acted that way." Dylan fell into his chair.

"You're worried about your family and your ranch. Anyone would be."

"I'm going to hire some temporary hands. I sent Monster with the boys, so adding some guard dogs would help. I might as well buy some with all the trouble that seems to come to the Rocking W. Usually on the heels of a woman." He rubbed his hands down his face. "I know you will be watching for the guy, but keep a close eye on Kentley. Moss wants her bad."

"I'll do everything in my power to keep her safe." Clay whipped around and returned to the bunkhouse to shower and change before the town meeting.

Getting the citizens involved, letting them know the town had an arsonist on the loose, might be the very thing to help the authorities bring Moss to justice. The more wary eyes, the better in his opinion.

He'd lived in Misty Hollow long enough to know of the prior troubles that had plagued the town. The residents always rallied together to protect their own. Kentley became one of them the day she started work on the ranch. At breakfast, he let her know about the meeting. They left the ranch at eight-thirty, both wearing a gun on their hip.

"You really think this will help?" She cut him a glance.

"Yes." No. "I don't know, but it's worth a try." He reached for her hand. "Anything is worth a try if it will keep you safe."

"If it will keep everyone safe." She slipped her hand free and stared out the window. "I'm not the only one in danger here."

"Don't pull away from me, Kentley. We're in this together, remember?" A feeling of rejection washed over him.

"I wish we weren't," she said softly.

"I don't." He reached for her hand again, pained when she pulled back. If they didn't catch Moss soon, he might not get the chance to see whether he and Kentley had a future together. Clay would get the chance to tell her out he felt about her. She'd be gone before he could. He knew that as sure as if she'd spoken the words out loud.

The parking lot of the sheriff's office was shoulder to shoulder with town residents. Clay parked his truck on the street and slid from his seat. Kentley exited before he could round the vehicle to open her door.

At precisely nine a.m., Sheriff Westbrook stood in front of a microphone and called for attention. "Thank you all for coming. These are Special Agents Snowe and Larson from the FBI. They have something of importance to say to the citizens of Misty Hollow."

Murmurs rose from the crowd.

Snowe took the sheriff's place. "Ladies and gentlemen, it is time to alert you to the fact that an arsonist is responsible for the recent fires around Misty Hollow. There are fliers by the front door with the photo of the man we believe to be responsible. Ryan Moss, a recent firefighter of your town. We are asking for your help in locating this man. If you see him, please call the sheriff's office. Do not approach him or try to detain him. Ryan Moss is armed and dangerous."

Dave Wakes, the big burly leader of the local biker club, spoke up. "Me and the guys will keep a look out.

You can count on us."

Snowe smiled. "Yes, you've been a big help in the past. Just remember…do not take the law into your own hands."

A reporter from the local paper raised her hand. "Is there a motive?"

Snowe hesitated before answering. "We believe he has an agenda, yes, but we don't think now is the time to release that information."

"So, he is targeting someone in this town?"

"No comment. No further questions. Please take a flyer before you leave." Snowe turned from the microphone and followed Larson into the building.

"Why doesn't he want anyone to know Moss is after me?" Kentley asked.

"You?" The reporter turned and thrust a microphone in her face.

Clay stepped protectively in front of her. "No comment." He put a hand on the small of Kentley's back and tried ushering her toward the truck.

She shrugged him off and raised her voice. "I will lead a town meeting this afternoon at five at Lucy's Diner. Anyone interested in helping, please come." With a defiant glance at Clay, she marched for his truck.

"Kentley," the sheriff growled.

"Arrest me if you want to stop me," she said without turning around.

Clay shot the sheriff a shocked look, then shrugged. "I'll try and talk some sense into her."

"She won't listen. I'll be there." With a shake of his head, he followed the agents into the building.

Clay returned to his truck and stared at Kentley.

"You're trying to stir things up so Moss comes for you soon, aren't you?"

She tilted her head and offered a rueful smile. "Let's see if it works."

Things were about to get very bad.

Chapter Fourteen

Lucy crossed her arms and narrowed her eyes while listening to Kentley explain the upcoming town meeting to be held in her diner. "An arsonist. And you want to hold the meeting here?" She exhaled heavily. "I won't say no because I'm always willing to help, but I sure pray this Moss character doesn't turn his attention on my diner. It's been in my family for a very long time."

Kentley would pray the same. "If you'd rather we didn't, we can use the high school gym…maybe."

"And burn down the school?" Her eyebrows rose to her dyed red hair. "No, we'll keep it here. I'll hire a security guard until this is over. I'd best go fill several pots of coffee. You're sure to have a crowd." She turned and headed for the kitchen.

"Am I wrong?" Kentley turned to Clay.

"In holding a meeting?" He shook his head. "I've thought for a while that the townsfolk needed to know about Moss. The way I see it, the more eyes looking for him, the better our chances of flushing him into the open."

"I'll never forgive myself if the diner is hit."

"I'm sure Dave and his biker buddies will make

sure that doesn't happen." He grinned. "Those dudes helped bring down organized crime once. They can handle Moss."

She sure hoped so.

At five o'clock, the ranch hands arrived, then the group of bikers, followed by enough town residents that it was standing room only in the diner. Kentley stood on a step stool behind the lunch counter and waited until the crowd had settled down with their coffee before beginning her speech. Perspiration beaded on her upper lip. She wasn't a public speaker. Never had been. Kentley glanced at Clay for help when the crowd kept talking among themselves.

He put two fingers to his lips and let out a shrill whistle loud enough to be heard in Langley thirty miles away. "Quiet, folks. Kentley has something you'll all want to hear."

She took a deep breath. "I'm Kentley Montgomery, and I work at the Rocking W. Trouble followed me here, and for that I am very sorry. I'm asking for your help in stopping Ryan Moss from burning down this town. He's already killed one man, and I have no doubt he won't hesitate to kill again."

The murmuring started again.

She held up her hand and waited for silence. "The FBI held a meeting outside the sheriff's office this morning, but they can't do this alone. It's going to take all of us. Who here is willing to help?"

The room erupted as shouts of 'yes' and 'you bet' rose. Kentley grinned so big her cheeks hurt. Together, they'd bring Moss to justice—of that she had no doubt.

"What's the plan, girl?" Dave stepped up.

"I'm going to…make myself available."

"Not without me and my buddies, you aren't."

She glanced at Clay who arched a brow and smiled. "I'm counting on all of you to keep me safe. Ryan Moss wants me to be cleansed by fire."

"Burned, you mean?"

"Yes. I'm not keen on that happening." She held out a hand and let the big man help her from the step stool.

"We take care of our own. Trust me, we've got your back. All of us." He glanced around the room where more shouts rose and heads nodded.

"Watch out for the diner, too," she said, more grateful for the support than she could say.

"We'll guard the place. Moss won't know we're here." He clapped a big hand on her shoulder, then joined his buddies on the other side of the room.

Tears burned her eyes. She'd found a place to belong, here in Misty Hollow—something she'd never had before. Her gaze drifted to Clay. Not only a place, but a person she could see herself forming a future with. Maybe. Once the danger was past. Kentley finally had something she never thought she'd have, and she'd be darned if she'd let Ryan take that away from her.

"You did good." Clay gave her a quick hug. "Moss won't be able to make a move without someone seeing him."

"That's what I hope will happen." Tears again filled her eyes at the support.

"Let's squeeze into a table and grab something to eat." Clay led her to a table for two near the kitchen. "Try the fried pork chops. You won't regret it."

She'd spotted the day's supper special when they'd entered the diner. "I don't think I could eat it all."

"Save some for tomorrow, since we're all responsible for feeding ourselves right now." He sat across from her as the harried waitress headed their way.

"Lucy doesn't have enough help for a crowd this big," the girl said. "What can I get you to drink?"

"Water," Kentley said. "I think we're both having the special."

"That comes with tea. Want sweet or unsweet?"

"Unsweet, please."

"Half and half for me." Clay smiled.

"Good thing you put your order in now. We're going to run out of the special." She rushed away.

Kentley folded her hands on the table and locked gazes with Clay. "We've got people looking out for Moss. Now we need a plan to draw him out. I can't exactly start taking nightly strolls down Main Street."

"I could text him."

She immediately chilled as if someone had dumped ice water over her head. "Do you think that would work?"

"Maybe. Or he could think it's a trap."

The waitress returned with their tea. Kentley's hand shook as she reached to take a drink. "I'm terrified."

"You should be. This could go very wrong."

~

Ryan stared across the street at the crowd inside the diner. No one paid any attention to the old man in overalls sitting on a bench outside the drugstore. No one questioned why he wasn't at the meeting. Who would think an old man useful in catching an arson? He laughed.

If they only knew how close he was.

Ryan eyed the motorcycles parked out front. He'd read the newspapers. It wouldn't be the FBI he needed to watch out for; it would be the bikers. A fiercely loyal group that would do anything to keep the streets of their town safe.

No matter. Ryan stood and meandered down the street. He knew how to be a ghost when he needed to. Just like tonight. Ryan knew how to be anyone, anything, when he needed to blend in or hide in plain sight.

He returned to his truck he'd parked in the alley behind the drugstore and drove to the vacant strip mall he'd made a temporary home in. The place had bathrooms, even if the toilets didn't flush. An old mattress left behind. He'd stolen blankets off a clothesline and a gas lantern from someone's back porch. Not exactly the Ritz, but he didn't plan on needing the place for long.

I'm coming for you, Kentley. Real soon.

~

Clay didn't know why he'd mentioned texting Moss. The man wasn't stupid. He'd know it was a trap. Still, it might spur the man into action—something Clay both wanted and dreaded. Somehow, he needed to make sure that he was there when Moss came for Kentley. Even if he stayed out of sight, he could follow them, stop him—something, anything, to keep Kentley out of the fire. He stared at the half-eaten meal in front of him, his appetite gone. Kentley wasn't the only one who would be taking leftovers home.

"What?" She peered over the rim of her glass.

"Nothing. Just thinking and having second

thoughts about the text."

"If not that, then what?" She set her glass down.

"Someday, I want to take you on a real date. One where we dress up and enjoy each other's company without the threat of a madman."

"That would be nice. Don't change the subject. We need a plan."

"I don't have one." He motioned for the waitress to bring two to-go boxes. "Other than keeping you alive, that is."

"I don't plan on letting Ryan kill me." She narrowed her eyes.

Folks filed past the table offering their help to Kentley and reassuring her that she wasn't alone. She smiled and thanked them, her smile fading as Sheriff Westbrook marched their way.

"Kentley. Clay. Mind if I sit?"

Clay scooted over. "Were you here the whole time?"

"Yep. Hid in the kitchen so I wouldn't have to answer too many questions." He sat next to Clay. "I was hoping to spot Moss hovering somewhere but didn't catch sight of the man. I know he had to be close. It wouldn't be like him not to want to watch the show."

"Is that what you thought of my meeting?" Kentley frowned.

"No. I'm only saying that most crooks visit the scene of the crime. We know he's been close to the fires. Why not here?" He removed his hat and set it on the table.

"You hungry?" Clay motioned at the uneaten pork chop.

"Haven't had time to eat all day. Thanks." He

pulled the plate in front of him. "You come up with a plan yet?"

"No. Has the FBI?"

He shook his head. "We're all running around in the dark like blind mice."

Kentley giggled. "That makes you doubly blind."

"Feels that way." He glanced out the window to where most of the crowd from inside had gathered. "I don't like that all these yahoos are now on a mission to catch Moss. Someone is going to be hurt or killed."

"We didn't see another way of getting to him," Clay said. "It's better if we take the control rather than leave it in his hands."

"It is in Moss's hands." He stabbed the pork chop as if it was the culprit. "The man is always ahead of us, and we're stumbling around trying to catch up."

"Surely you've seen his like before." He'd been FBI once.

"Yep, but we don't always get the bad guy." He glanced at Kentley. "Sometimes, we don't save the target."

She hitched her chin. "Then it's up to me to save myself."

"Let's pray you do." He finished Clay's meal and stood. "Keep me up-to-date, and I'll share what I can. Stay safe."

"He's worried." Kentley's gaze followed the sheriff.

"Yep, and that doesn't fill me with reassurance." After Kentley slid the uneaten portion of her meal into the box, Clay escorted her outside.

The local reporter met them at the door. "Can I ask you a few questions?"

"Everything that needed saying was said inside." Clay tried to skirt around the woman, keeping an arm around Kentley's waist.

Honey popped her big head out of the truck window and sniffed the box in Kentley's hand.

"You want this, sweetie? Then wait until we get home." Kentley kissed the dog between the eyes and told her to get back so she could climb in.

The reporter asked again for a comment, then spun around and stormed away when Clay and Kentley ignored her.

Clay climbed into the driver's seat and waited as a car blocked him as he backed away. The roar of motorcycles filled the air and filed in behind him as he left the parking lot.

"Looks like they're following us to the ranch." Kentley turned in her seat.

"From what I've heard, they take their job very seriously." Good. He had help in keeping Kentley safe, and it would be harder for her to sneak away with those men watching.

As he turned into the winding drive of the Rocking W, the motorcycles turned around and headed back down the mountain. To protect the diner, Clay hoped. Kentley was right to be worried. Moss might retaliate against the town by burning down one of its landmarks. He glanced sideways at Kentley. One more thing she'd blame on herself.

The other ranch hands milled around in front of the main house. Clay turned off the ignition and climbed out of the truck. "What's up?"

Willy crossed his arms. "We've got a plan."

Chapter Fifteen

A plan? "Let's hear it." Excitement leaped within. Finally, Kentley might see an end to Moss's reign of terror.

"A picnic." Willy grinned.

"A picnic?" Kentley and Clay asked in unison.

"Yep. At the lake. We tell a few people in town. Word spreads like fire, pardon the pun, and voilà." He snapped his fingers. "Moss is bound to show up to snatch our Kentley."

Our Kentley. She'd never tire of hearing those words. "Okay, when?"

"Tomorrow night. We're already spreading the word. We thought night was best so Moss feels like he can blend in and hide better." Willy seemed very proud of himself, his weathered face beaming. "Don't worry. We'll take care of everything."

"Have you alerted the authorities?" Clay frowned.

"They'll hear the same as everyone else."

Kentley glanced at Dylan who watched from the porch. "You agree?"

He shrugged. "You want to face him, so let's face him. I'd like to bring my family home." He glanced at each of those gathered. "I want everyone armed. No one lets Kentley out of their sight. Got it?"

Heads nodded and Clay stepped closer to her side. Kentley had never felt more safe in her life. She rubbed her hands together. "Let's do this."

She didn't think she'd be able to sleep that night with her mind whirling in anticipation over what might be the end of Moss, but the sun woke her from a deep sleep the next morning. She stretched and yawned, then climbed from bed and padded to the window.

Two German shepherds she'd never seen before sniffed around the yard. A man with burn scars on his face and a woman spoke to Dylan on the back deck. That must be the foreman, Maverick, and his wife back from a search-and-rescue case. She'd heard the men talking about them. Good. Two more to keep an eye out for Moss. At first, the sight of the man's scars had sent trickles of fear down her spine until she'd realized he wasn't Ryan.

She quickly got dressed and joined them on the deck, introducing herself.

Maverick squared his shoulders. "I feel the need to let you know I'm afraid of fire."

"That makes two of us." She thrust out her hand. "Nice to meet you."

"I'm Blair," the woman said. "Don't worry about us. We've been through the fire before and come out just fine." She smiled up at her husband. "He's a lot braver than he lets on."

Maverick grinned. "I do enjoy a good picnic, though."

"Are those your dogs?"

"Yes. We started with just one, but we're training another. Don't worry. They'll do just fine with your fur baby." Blair glanced at Honey who watched the other two dogs with interest. "Let me go help Willy plan the food for this picnic."

As they all headed to their own plans for the morning, Kentley went to the barn to fetch Stormy and lead her through her paces. She rode the horse every day, even if only around the paddock, in order to form a trust between the two of them.

The horse nickered a welcome.

"Hello, beautiful." She pressed her forehead against the horse's muzzle. "Ready for some exercise before I muck out the stalls?"

The horse nudged her with her head and snorted.

"Great. Me, too." Kentley quickly saddled the horse and led her from the barn.

She did her best not to dwell on the upcoming picnic, but trickles of fear ran through her at the thought of seeing Moss face-to-face. Maybe. If she was lucky…or would that be unlucky? Either way, she tried to force the nervousness away and focus on her job until it was time to go. By the time she joined Clay at his truck, her stomach had twisted in knots. "I'm more worried than I thought I would be."

"Good. You should be scared spitless." He opened the passenger side door for her. "Tonight might not end as we'd like."

"Don't be so pessimistic. I need your reassurance." She climbed in after Honey.

"Sorry," he said once he sat in the driver's seat. "Promise me you'll be vigilant." He cupped her cheek, his palm rough on her skin. "I'll do my best to protect you, but if I can't—"

"I'll do my best to protect *you*." She closed her

eyes and leaned into his touch.

"Hmm." He pulled away and started the truck.

Kentley stared out her window as they drove to the lake. What if Moss didn't show? The place would be crawling with armed cowboys, deputies, and FBI agents. She'd have to find a way to step away by herself in order for him to feel safe enough to emerge.

It wouldn't be easy with Clay glued to her side. Would Moss come if Clay was with her? Should she try? It would be safer for her, maybe, but it could put Clay in mortal danger. Moss didn't want him. Kentley was his only target. Everyone else was collateral damage.

Clay parked next to Dylan's truck. Kentley slid from the vehicle and held the door for Honey. "You stay with me, girl."

"I plan on it, too." Clay put a hand on her back. "If you even go to the restroom, I'll be right outside the door."

"At least you aren't going in with me." She tried not to let her nervousness show but failed when her voice shook.

He chuckled. "I'll let Honey go with you."

"Thanks." She gave a short laugh as they approached the others.

The sun started to set over the horizon, highlighting the lake's surface with hints of gold. The trees' shadows stretched over the surface. A family of ducks paddled by. "Why have I not been in this beautiful spot before?"

"You've been preoccupied. I'll bring you on a picnic with just the two of us someday."

She really hoped they would get the chance.

Soon, the aroma of grilling burgers mingled with the sweet summer breeze. Laughter filled the air. Kentley could almost forget the real reason they were all there. Until the sheriff and the FBI agents arrived to remind her.

"We don't like this," Snowe said.

"Too dangerous," Larson added.

"And too late to stop it." Kentley tilted her head. "Have a burger, enjoy yourselves, and let's see how this plays out."

"You could be dead at the end of this party, ma'am." Larson shook his head.

"Then that would be the end of Moss, too." She marched to the water's edge.

Yes, she could die that night, but she had the same chance of not dying. She'd take the fifty-fifty odds.

Her gaze traveled the path leading around the lake. Where are you, Ryan? With a backward glance, she headed for the path, motioning for Honey to follow her while Clay argued with the FBI agents.

Soon, the darkness of the woods swallowed her. The birds quieted. The silence made the hair on Kentley's arms stand at attention.

Honey growled.

A twig snapped.

Kentley whirled as Ryan stepped from the shadows.

"Strange to see you out here alone." His eyes glittered in what little moonlight filtered through the tree branches. "Unless you came to see me?"

"I did."

"This isn't the time. I have something grand planned for you." His gaze switched to Honey. "It involves your dog, but someone else, too."

"This involves no one else." She put a protective hand on Honey's head.

"Oh, but it does. You need to want to be a hero bad enough to do what I ask of you."

"Why are you doing this? I was kind to you. Grateful that you saved my dog."

He slapped his neck. "I hate mosquitos." He gave a long, slow exhale. "When you hugged me that day, I knew we were meant to be together always. But, I'm a hero, you know." He ran his hand over his scars. "I need you to be a hero, too."

"You don't plan on letting me live."

"No, we'll both have to perish, but you'll have proven your worth before you do. Folks around here will remember you always. They'll tell stories about your heroic action and sad demise."

The man was seriously demented. "I don't want to be a hero."

"It's your destiny."

"Then let's do it now." She took a step toward him.

"No!" His voice rose. "We do this when the time is right. I still have things to do."

"Kentley!" Clay's panicked voice rang through the trees.

"Soon, though." Ryan darted back into the shadows as Clay burst into view.

"What are you doing?" Clay gripped her arms. "You know you shouldn't go off alone."

"He was here. I spoke to him." She searched his face through the darkness, then gripped his hand. "We must go."

"Now, you're in a hurry?"

"He's going to use you and Honey as bait to coerce me to do as he says. We can't be together, Clay."

~

Wait. What? "He's going to use me?"

"Yes. We have to get back to the others."

Once they returned to the festivities, he faced her. "Why did you go alone, knowing the danger? You scared me to death."

"I want this to end. It's going to be so much worse than I thought. He wants me to save you and Honey."

Clay froze. She was right. They couldn't stay together. He would have to watch his back—make sure Moss didn't get to him. "We need to let the sheriff know."

"Yes. You need round-the-clock protection."

The sheriff and agents listened as Kentley told them of her conversation with Moss.

Dylan shot Clay a wide-eyed glance. "I don't want you leaving the ranch for anything. Moss won't come for you there. If he does, shoot him."

"Hold on." Sheriff Westbrook held up his hands. "I agree Clay needs to stay under the protection of the ranch, but no one is shooting anyone."

"I won't hesitate if the opportunity presents itself." Clay crossed his arms. "He plans on killing Kentley. He doesn't want me dead. He plans on her saving me. The only two he plans on being dead at the end of this is Moss and Kentley. I don't plan on it being her."

"Both of you need to go to a safe house," Snowe said. "We have one in Eureka Springs—"

"No." Kentley shook her head. "He'll use the citizens of Misty Hollow to force us back. I can't have that on my head."

"Then both of you don't leave the ranch."

"What about our duties at the fire house?" Clay asked.

"They'll have to borrow firemen from somewhere else." The sheriff glanced from Kentley to Clay. "It's the only way to keep you safe."

"I won't hide." Clay refused to be intimidated. "But, I will agree not to leave the ranch without at least two ranch hands with me."

"Same goes for me," Kentley said. "If he doesn't see me with Clay anymore, he might change his plan."

"And come for you." No way would he allow that.

"Yes." She jutted out her chin.

"The two of you can argue about this at the ranch. This picnic is over." Dylan marched away telling everyone to pack up and head back.

"You're the most stubborn woman…" Clay sighed.

"And you're the most hardheaded man." She grinned. "We make a good pair."

Her laughter shocked him into doing the same. "Yes, we are. Let's pray we can explore how well that works for us in the future."

"I'm not usually obstinate." She gazed up at him. "I don't want anything to happen to you. Ryan is right. I'd walk into the fire to save you."

Which scared Clay more.

Chapter Sixteen

Kentley had been going about the whole fiasco with Ryan in the wrong way. It wasn't a surprise that he would use Honey to lure her. He knew how much the dog meant to Kentley. It didn't take a genius to see how much she'd grown to care for Clay.

She'd been foolish enough to believe he'd use the town of Misty Hollow rather than one person. Kentley lifted her coffee cup to her lips and watched as Clay wheeled a load of manure toward the garden mulch pile.

Sweat glistened on his bare back. Muscles rippled. Had God ever made a more perfect specimen? She doubted it. Now, she'd jeopardized everything.

What she should have done was flee the mountain at the first hint of trouble. She was used to being alone…once. Now, the thought of being alone again filled her with overwhelming sadness. So, what to do? If she wanted to keep this family she'd found, how could she succeed?

Ryan wouldn't come into the open again unless it was to grab Clay and Honey. An almost impossible task considering they were constantly surrounded by at least two ranch hands at every given moment. Waiting for

Ryan to make a move made every nerve in her body twang. She'd rather be the one in control and not succumb to the whims of a madman.

The clang of the dinner bell startled her. It wasn't time for a meal. Her coffee mug slipped from her fingers and shattered on the wooden deck. Hot coffee splashed on her ankles. She jumped to her feet with a gasp as everyone sprinted for the front of the house.

"Come, Honey." Kentley leaped from the deck and rushed to join the others.

"Make haste, everyone," Dylan said. "The diner is on fire."

Oh, no. Kentley's greatest fear. Her meeting to get the townsfolk involved had jeopardized the town's treasure.

"Stop blaming yourself." Clay glared over the top of the truck.

"I wasn't."

"Liar." He gave a quick grin and climbed in the driver's seat.

Seconds later, they sped down the mountain with the others. *Please, God, don't let the diner be a loss*, she prayed.

Vehicles and spectators clogged Main Street. Two firemen aimed their hoses on the blaze. The hands of Misty Hollow grabbed blankets and shovels from their truck beds and rushed to help.

Kentley did what she always did at a fire, even though she knew what she and Honey would find. She wasn't mistaken as she glanced down at the gas can and matchbook. Ryan had struck again, making it more personal to Misty Hollow than ever. Hopefully, the fire could be contained to the front of the building.

She glanced at the crowd. He had to be there somewhere, close—maybe in disguise.

A heavily bearded, overweight man in overalls stood off to one side, his hands shoved into his pockets. Kentley narrowed her eyes. Most of the people conversed among themselves, yet this man stood alone. "Clay?" She jerked her head toward the man.

"Yeah?"

"I think that's Moss."

He turned in the direction she motioned. "You think so?"

"Gut feeling."

Clay huffed. "Now what? He can't exactly abduct me with all these people around."

"I think he's making a point that he can get close." She had taken a step toward the man, when he tapped his forefinger against the rim of his baseball cap and strolled away from the fire.

"Sheriff!" One of the bike riders yelled out. "Over here. It's Ben."

With a quick glance at Clay, Kentley followed the sheriff to the small stand of trees next to the diner. One of the bikers lay in the shade, a knife protruding from his chest.

Dave hurried behind her and cursed. "He was a good man and didn't deserve this. All he wanted to do was protect the diner."

Clay clapped a hand on the big man's shoulder. "We'll get him." He described the man in overalls. "Maybe you can find him."

Dave nodded and whistled to attract the attention of his gang. "We've got a rat to catch."

Soon, the roar of engines filled the air as the bikers

filed down Main Street in search of Moss. Kentley almost envied them, wishing she could go with them.

Shouts of "Go get him!" and "Hang him up!" followed the bikers as the town citizens voiced their feelings.

Kentley caught sight of Lucy and her husband across the street and headed that way. "I'm so sorry." She swallowed the lump in her throat.

"Not your fault."

"It is. You were afraid this would happen."

Lucy tore her gaze from the fire to Kentley. "You didn't start the fire, dear. I've got insurance. We'll rebuild bigger and better. You'll see."

"Looks like the kitchen will be spared," her husband said. "That's a blessing. We'll still be able to run the business with tables set up outside. We can make it work."

Kentley's lip quivered at their forced optimism. "Again, I'm truly sorry."

Lucy gave a sad smile. "Let me know when you catch the guy. I've a few words to say to the murdering scoundrel. It's sad about Ben. I really hope Ryan Moss is behind bars very soon for the sake of this town. The man is like a wraith slipping in and out of the shadows. This time he struck in daylight."

The more the woman talked, the worse Kentley felt, but she wouldn't stop her. Lucy had a right to voice her opinion, and talking could start the healing process.

"Your man is waiting for you," Lucy said, pointing Kentley's attention to Clay.

He wasn't her man, but she sure wanted him to be. She headed back across the street.

~

Ryan climbed into his truck a few blocks over and sped from town, leaving the sound of motorcycle engines behind. He hadn't meant to kill the biker, but the man had caught him starting the fire and attacked him. What alternative did he have but to drive the knife into his chest? Besides, who cared about one biker in the grand scheme of things? Ryan was a hero and had a destiny. One that involved Kentley. Burning the diner was nothing more than another step toward his goal.

Step two—Get the townspeople riled up. Worked into a frenzy. They'd all be so fired up to catch him they'd run willy-nilly around Misty Hollow and the mountain without a clear plan on locating him.

Ryan spewed out a laugh. He'd been staying under their noses for weeks now. A few more targets to hit, a few more taunts to the cowboy, and he'd be ready to make his final move. All he had to do was watch for the opportunity and pounce.

~

"I got a text." Clay held out his phone for Kentley to read while he did the same out loud. "*I see you. I'm coming for you.*"

"That's almost like the one he sent me." She stared at him with wide eyes.

"I've already let the sheriff know and described the man in overalls. People are looking for him, but I'm pretty sure he'll wear a different disguise next time." It was like looking for a particular shell on the beach.

"Are you going to reply?"

He grinned. "I told him to bring it."

"Oh, Clay."

He held out his arms, and she stepped into them.

The man she loved rested his chin on top of her head. "This won't stop until he gets me."

"You might end up like Ben."

"Nah. You'll save me, then we'll bring him down together. I plan on dying as an old man, at home in my own bed, while my beautiful wife holds my hand."

She let out a short laugh. "Big dreams."

"Absolutely."

She peered up at him. "And where does this dream take place?"

"On a ranch. Someday, I plan on owning my own place. It isn't hard to save living rent free in the bunkhouse. What are your dreams, Kentley?"

"To have a family of my own. I'm already there." She rested her cheek against his chest, and he tightened his hold on her.

Yes, she had that family she dreamed of, and he was a part of it. He didn't plan on letting her go, Moss or not. One day, they'd face the man together and come out the victors. Maybe scarred, but stronger because of it. Then, Clay would ask the woman in his arms to stick around and be part of his dream.

He wanted to ask her now, but he couldn't. While he didn't think he'd die at the hands of Moss, Clay had no guarantee, and he wouldn't leave her grieving too long by forming a more permanent relationship with her.

"We're heading back." Dylan broke them up. "The fire is under control. The kitchen still stands. It's time to get you two back to the protection of the ranch."

Clay nodded and led Kentley back to the truck. With ranch hands driving in front of them and in back, they returned to the Rocking W.

"My arrival here has disrupted everyone's schedule." Kentley glanced behind them.

"It isn't the first time trouble has come to Misty Hollow."

"Maybe not, but this time it followed me." She huffed. "No more pity parties. We're going to end this."

He reached for her hand and gave it a gentle squeeze. "That's my girl."

Her cheeks turned a pretty shade of pink. "I like the sound of that."

So did he, and he planned on kissing her before the day ended.

As the sun set over Misty Mountain, he followed Kentley and Stormy into the barn. Once the horse had been taken care of for the night, Clay grinned.

"What?" Kentley frowned.

"I'm going to kiss you. It's all I've thought of this afternoon." He stepped forward.

She arched a brow. "You aren't going to ask?"

"Nope. I don't want you to say no."

"I wouldn't," she said softly.

He removed her hair from its braid and let the curls fall down her back. Entwining his fingers in the red tresses, he pulled her close and claimed her lips.

She tasted of sugar, heaven, and dreams.

He deepened the kiss, reveling in the slight moan that escaped her. This was what he wanted. This woman right here. He'd do everything in his power to make sure he wouldn't lose her.

Chapter Seventeen

The fierce barking of the two German shepherds had Kentley bolting from bed the next morning. Honey stood at the window, hackles raised, making deep noises in her throat.

Kentley grabbed her gun from her nightstand, slipped her feet into sandals, then raced from her room to the back deck. Ranch hands saddled horses, shouting to each other. She turned as Clay exited the barn with his horse and Stormy.

"I hope you can herd cattle." He handed her the reins.

"What happened?" She stuffed the gun in the back waistband of the shorts she'd slept in and climbed into the saddle. Could she herd? She didn't know, never having done so.

"Back fence has been cut, and the cows are blocking traffic on the main road across the mountain." He swung into his saddle with ease.

Hooves shook the ground and kicked up dirt as they galloped to the road. Chaos reigned as more than just the Rocking W cattle converged on the road.

A neighboring rancher, Rick Millsap, rode toward them. "Fences cut all over this mountain. It's madness."

"Pranksters or Moss?" Kentley glanced at Clay.

"I'm going with Moss."

Her heart jumped to her throat. Was this how he intended to grab Clay and Honey? They could easily be taken while separating the Rocking W herd from the others.

"This isn't the only place trouble is brewing," another rancher said. "Power lines cut in town. The streetlights aren't working, and someone opened several of the fire hydrants from what I've heard. Someone was very busy last night."

Kentley frowned. If Ryan was behind this, then why cause havoc both on the mountain and in town? It didn't make sense.

Dylan shouted for his hands to start separating the Rocking W cattle. It didn't take long for Kentley and Clay to be separated. With the yells of cowboys and mooing of cattle, she couldn't pick out Clay's voice from the others.

Kentley raised up in her stirrups to locate him. Her heart raced until she spotted him on the other side of the herd. She didn't see how Ryan could reach him with so many people around, but the man had proven to be bolder than any of them thought. To cut fencing and cause havoc in town took a lot of guts and planning. Preventing him from dragging her into the fire with him would be next to impossible. The man seemed like a mastermind.

She promptly lost sight of Clay again as cattle jostled Stormy. The horse reared. Kentley held on tight to prevent sliding off and being trampled. The horse danced sideways, eyes rolling in fear.

Kentley patted her neck until she calmed, then

guided her out of the throng. Stormy was too new for the job of herding. All she could do was try and keep the cattle from splitting off and running into the woods.

Was Ryan watching and laughing? The disorganized job of separating cattle had to be humorous to him. Or was he in town watching the insanity there?

So much mayhem, both in Misty Hollow and here, played in her mind. She searched the crowd again for Clay. When she couldn't find him, her heart seized. She rode Stormy up and down the road, searching for his familiar face. "Find Clay, Honey." She hated to let the dog out of her sight.

What if Ryan took them both? Would today be the day he beckoned Kentley to him by taking those she loved? Tears blurred her vision as Honey darted between the cows. She could lose both of them that day.

No. She refused to think that way. They would get through this together even if they faced Ryan. Somehow, someway, they'd survive and put an end to his reign of terror. The alternative was too frightening to comprehend.

There he was! She breathed a sigh of relief to see Clay and Honey heading her way.

"Your furry girl fetched me." He smiled and leaned on the saddle horn.

"I couldn't see you."

"Don't worry, darlin'. You've been in my sight the whole time."

"Ryan wants you first."

"True, but I doubt he'll grab me with all this—" He waved his arm. "I won't be so easily taken, Kentley."

"Yeah, I know. I'm just scared." She sniffed. "I'm trying not to worry, but when I can't see you…"

"I'll make sure to stay close. Let me finish up here so we can get back to the ranch." He turned his horse back to the job, leaving her feeling silly for worrying.

Clay was right. They couldn't be safer than when surrounded by a bunch of cowboys carrying weapons.

~

Clay's smile faded the moment he turned around. Kentley was right to be worried. This was the perfect time for Ryan to come. Keep everyone preoccupied— this was probably the man's plan. Keep everyone hyper focused, then sneak in and grab.

It made it hard for him to do his job and keep an eye out for Moss at the same time. The other ranch hands had his back, but they were busy, too. With the trouble in town, the sheriff and deputies wouldn't be coming to the mountain. It was up to the Rocking W and its neighbors to keep everyone safe.

The buzz of approaching motorcycles calmed his racing heart. Help was coming after all. His smile returned as he rode up to Dave.

"It's good to see you all."

Dave nodded. "Some of us stayed to help in town, but we thought you could use some help. We'll block off both ends of the road to keep the cattle from spreading out further. Anything else we can help with?"

"I don't think so, but I'll send Dylan over. He's in charge. Thanks for coming." He steered his horse to Dylan who agreed Dave's plan would be a big help.

After letting the biker know, Clay headed his horse after an escaping calf who ventured toward the thick foliage of the forest. Once the calf was back with its group, he went back to work, separating those with the Rocking W brand from the rest of the cattle. Not an easy task, but after a couple of hours, all the cattle were separated and herded back to the prospective ranches.

"Put them in the horse paddock until we repair the fence," Dylan said.

"Want some of us to head into town?" Willy asked.

"No. Our priority is this ranch and those who live here." Dylan bent and opened the paddock gate so the cows could be driven in.

"I'll go to where I'm better suited and fix sandwiches." Kentley slid from the saddle and led her horse toward the barn.

"Sandwiches sound great." Clay held out his hand. "I'll take care of Stormy."

"Thanks." She flashed a smile through the dust on her face and hurried toward the main house.

A few minutes later, she returned with a knife in one hand and a sheet of paper in the other. "We've had a visitor." She handed the paper to Clay.

He read, "*Isn't this fun?*"

He frowned. "Moss was in the house?"

"We left in such a hurry the back door must've been left unlocked." Dylan's face darkened. "We need to search the house."

"He'll be long gone." Clay pulled his weapon.

"Most likely, but we still need to look." Together, leaving the other hands to care for the cattle, the two marched for the house.

Kentley followed.

"I'd rather you stay out here," Clay tossed over his shoulder.

"You might need backup. Ryan isn't after Dylan;

he's after you." Her expression left no room for argument.

"Fine, but stay close." He eyed the gun in her hand and huffed.

The three of them entered a silent house that usually rang out with the laughter and shouts of the twins and the chatter of Marilyn and Mrs. White in the kitchen. Now, the large house seemed eerie as Clay and Kentley headed up the stairs, leaving the downstairs for Dylan.

They searched each room thoroughly and found no other evidence Moss had been there.

"I found the note stuck to the kitchen island with the knife," Kentley said. "Mrs. White isn't going to be happy about the gouge."

"We'll fix it before she returns." Grateful not to have found Moss hiding in any of the rooms, Clay returned his gun to the holster on his hip. *Isn't this fun? Far from it, you insane goon.* He stared down at Kentley's beautiful, freckled face. "He's getting too close."

"Yes," she said, her voice husky. "He must've cut the Rocking W fence last. The dogs barking woke me."

"Then, he waited in the woods for us to leave before entering the house."

"At least he didn't burn the house down." She spun around and headed back downstairs.

Clay frowned. He'd wanted to kiss her again, to ground himself with something wonderful. Instead, he joined her and Dylan outside where the boss spoke to the other ranch hands.

"Moss knows your patrolling schedule. This has to stop. We need to prevent him from stepping foot on this ranch." Dylan crossed his arms. "Don't patrol on a schedule. Don't circle the property. Move back and forth in teams of two. We'll work in shifts during the day and night. There won't be a lot of sleep for any of us. Clay and Kentley will not be on patrol at any time since they are the primary targets. Any questions?"

Heads shook.

"Good. Since he's already made himself known today, finish your chores and get some rest. Me and Willy will keep the first watch. Kentley, those sandwiches? And lots of coffee."

"On it." She darted back into the house.

Clay turned his attention to the thick woods at the end of the property. Moss flitted in and out like a wraith, spreading fear on the mountain and in the town. Where was he hiding? There were a lot of hunting cabins on the mountain, but he had to be somewhere close. In town, maybe. Someplace he could get in and out of quickly. "This is probably a dumb question." He turned to Dylan. "But has anyone checked all of the vacant buildings in and around town?"

"I hope the feds would have thought of that. It'll take a while, though. Misty Hollow hasn't grown in a few years. Lots of empty places where a man could hide."

Clay intended to ask the sheriff anyway. If they hadn't made it through the whole town, then they didn't have enough people searching. The sheriff wasn't an idiot. He'd have thought of that.

Clay's shoulders slumped. He needed to be proactive. Do something other than wait for Moss to show his face. He wanted to be the one searching for the man, to be the one who found him and ministered justice.

He glanced behind him. More than anything, he wanted to protect Kentley.

135

Chapter Eighteen

After two weeks of no fires, no chaos, and no messages or texts, Kentley woke in a state of confusion. Why would Ryan stop the torment?

Dylan spoke of bringing his family home, stating that Ryan must've been injured, ill, or better yet…dead. She didn't believe it possible. Even with the boss's words of the danger being over, her nerves stayed on edge. Ryan hadn't quit; he was simply holed up somewhere biding his time.

The aroma of frying bacon beckoned her to the kitchen where Willy, wearing one of Mrs. White's frilly aprons, fixed breakfast. He turned with a grin, a spatula in one hand. "Sheriff said they found where Moss had been holding up, but he's gone. Nothing left behind but some empty grocery bags and aluminum cans."

Clay entered the room, his hair still wet from his shower. "I don't believe it. The man is up to something."

"Well, regardless, it's been a nice reprieve. Sit. I made flapjacks and bacon to celebrate." Willy waved them toward the table.

"Let me help." Kentley opened the cupboard.

"Nothing to do. Table's all set."

With a shrug, she joined Clay at the table as the other ranch hands filed in, followed by Dylan. She glanced over at Clay. "What do you think Ryan is up to?"

"I don't know, but it scares me. He's waiting for us to let our guard down."

"That won't happen. Not for a long time or until he's behind bars."

"Or they find his body." He gave a wry smile. "One can always hope he had a heart attack, right?"

"You're so bad." She grinned. "I do agree it would be no great loss, but isn't every life worth something? Even his?"

"The bible says so. Forgive me, but I'm human enough to want the man gone permanently."

"I'm with Clay," Dylan said.

The other ranch hands offered their agreement in a series of grunts as they ate their food.

"You can't tell me that you wouldn't shoot to kill if he tried to murder Clay." Maverick crossed his arms.

"No, I never said that." Kentley met his hard gaze. "But, I won't kill because my emotions or anger propels me to." In fact, she prayed she'd never have to kill more than a spider. She hated spiders.

"Since things have been quiet," Clay whispered in her ear. "How about I take you on a real date tonight? To a restaurant in Langley."

His breath tickled the hair behind her ear, sending shivers down her spine. "That sounds nice."

"Great. Meet me out front at five-thirty."

Willy clapped Clay on the shoulder. "Just kiss her. You're wasting a prime opportunity."

Those at the table laughed and chanted, "kiss her,

kiss her."

Kentley's face heated. Her gaze locked with Clay's.

"I think I will," he whispered before pressing his lips to hers.

Hoots and hollers followed. She didn't think her face could get any hotter. So, she did the only thing she could think of and dug into her flapjacks.

After breakfast, she shooed Willy from the kitchen and started the cleanup. Clay grabbed a dishtowel.

"You wash and I'll dry."

"It'll take a while." She filled the sink with hot sudsy water.

"I have nothing better to do than wash dishes with you." The warm look in his eyes melted her heart.

Again at a loss for words, she turned away and plunged her hands into the water. "Hot!"

He reached over and turned on the cold tap. "Flustered?"

"You tend to do that to me."

He chuckled. "I hope I always do that to you."

As they worked side by side, he painted a picture of their future together.

Please, God, let it be so. "Do you think, if I should ever leave the ranch, that Dylan would let me buy Stormy?" She'd fallen in love with the horse, and the thought of not seeing her every day sent a pang through her heart.

"She'd be expensive." He dried a plate. "You thinking on leaving?"

"No, but no one knows what the future holds." If Clay bought his own ranch—if she were lucky enough to be asked to go with him—then she'd need a horse.

She didn't want any horse but Stormy.

"If that time should come, maybe he'll work out a deal with you. I don't like to talk about you leaving. This is your home."

More home than she'd ever had. "I don't have plans on leaving."

"Good. End of subject." He leaned over and planted a quick kiss on her cheek. "This place wouldn't be the same without you."

Later that afternoon, she stared into her closet at the one and only dress she'd brought with her. A sleeveless coral dress that reminded her of a sunset. The tag still dangled from the neckline. She'd fallen in love with the dress when she'd seen it in a shop window and bought it on impulse, never thinking she'd actually have a chance to wear it.

Kentley peered at the white sandals she'd only worn once. At least she wouldn't embarrass Clay at the restaurant. She dressed, put her hair into a French twist, applied a minimal amount of makeup, and headed downstairs to join him on the front porch, not feeling like herself at all, but feeling pretty for the first time in a long time.

He whistled at the sight of her. "Gorgeous."

"You clean up nice yourself." In black slacks and a royal-blue collared shirt, he could grace the cover of any magazine.

With a bow, he opened the passenger side door of his truck. "Your chariot awaits, my lady."

She giggled, told Honey she wasn't coming this time, and climbed inside, then arranged her dress around her knees. Her dog still stood, panting. "Sorry, girl. Three's a crowd tonight."

The dog sat and stared with forlorn eyes.

"I'll bring you back a doggy bag. You help hold down the fort here."

"She can go with me." Ryder marched toward them. "Me and River are your escorts. We promise to stay in the background, but them's the boss's orders. You don't leave the ranch without at least two of us with you."

~

Clay frowned. Although he knew the decision was wise, he'd really hoped to have a normal evening alone with Kentley. Someday.

He drove the half hour to Langley, mindful not to speed off and leave their escorts behind, no matter how much he wanted to. The absence of Moss didn't mean he was gone. It meant he was biding his time before making his next move.

He found a parking spot at the popular steak house, then hurried to open the door for Kentley, doing his best to ignore the two other ranch hands who parked a spot over.

"We'll be out here," River called. "Take your time."

"This is ridiculous," Kentley muttered. "They're going to attract attention."

"No, you'll do that when we walk in the door. You're beautiful." He smiled and opened the door to the restaurant. "Let's pretend they aren't out there. If we request a table away from the window, we should be fine. It's the view at the back of the restaurant we want to see anyway."

A hostess led them to a window overlooking the range of mountains stretching to the horizon. The lodge feel of the place lent to the romance.

Kentley sat and spread her napkin on her lap before opening her menu. Her eyes widened. "This place is expensive."

"The food is worth it, believe me. Order what you want." Clay smiled over the top of his menu. "I'm ordering the New York strip."

Kentley ordered the six-ounce filet with a loaded baked potato. "This is a nice place. Did you call for reservations?"

"I did. We wouldn't have gotten in otherwise." He reached over and took her hand. "How about a horseback ride and picnic tomorrow? Just the two of us and Honey."

"Plus an escort." She sighed and glanced out the window.

"We'll pretend we're celebrities and used to bodyguards." He gave her hand a gentle squeeze, relishing the way it fit his as if made to be there. "This will pass, sweetheart. We just have to hang in there."

"I know." She turned back to him with a smile. "I'm not going to think about Ryan. I want to enjoy tonight and tomorrow and the next day. What will come will come, and I hold onto the hope that the FBI will catch him soon."

"That's my girl."

The waitress brought them their meals and refilled their glasses of iced tea.

Despite wanting to stay in the moment, Clay couldn't forget about the two men standing guard outside and ordered burgers to be sent out to them, plus another for Honey.

"You're always thinking of others," Kentley said.

"I wish I was more like you."

"What do you mean?" He frowned. "You're one of the kindest people I know." His frown turned to a grin. "That's why we're in this mess, remember?"

"Ha ha." She laughed. "Who knew that a simple hug would send a madman into obsession."

"It's your beauty he's obsessed about."

"Stop it." She brought his hand to her lips. "Seriously, though, I had no idea."

"We aren't thinking about him, remember?"

"Right."

Still, the thought of Moss on the loose had to remain at the forefront of both their minds. At least for now.

After they'd eaten and he'd paid the bill, they drove back to the ranch. He half expected to hear that Moss had come out of hiding. When there was still no news, he didn't know whether to celebrate or worry.

Not wanting his evening with Kentley to end too soon, and refusing to spend any more time on Moss, he invited Kentley to the back deck for coffee. "The evening is too nice to end yet."

"Agreed. I've had a wonderful time."

"There are plenty more nights like this ahead of us. I promise." He darted into the house to make the coffee leaving her in the protection of Honey.

A few minutes later, a cup in each hand, he rejoined her. "Lots of vanilla cream."

"Just the way I like it. Thank you." She took the cup and breathed deep of the steam. "I'm so glad I'm not one of those people who can't have caffeine in the evening. It won't keep me awake at all."

"Good. We can sit long into the night."

"I know we said we wouldn't talk about Ryan, but…" She exhaled as if she'd been holding her breath for a long time. "We need to find out whether he's really gone."

"What do you suggest?" He settled into the chair next to her.

"I don't know." She stared toward the thick woods at the edge of the property. "If we don't find out, I'll spend the rest of my life looking over my shoulder."

"I agree, but I don't see how we can find him when the FBI can't." He checked his phone regularly thinking he might've missed a text from Moss, but nary a message had appeared in two weeks. "I think he's trying to rattle us. Maybe to get us to let down our guard."

"You don't think he's left?"

"No. You're still here. He's been pretty adamant about his plans for you." Clay cleared his throat, hating the reminder about the danger they were all in. "He won't stop. For some reason, he's gone quiet. He'll make himself known again at some point."

"I hope it isn't something horrible."

"Me, too." He took her hand, content to sit as the night cooled and the birds stilled. No other sound but the mooing of the cattle in the newly repaired pasture.

A full moon rose in an indigo sky. Stars twinkled. Everything was perfect.

Almost. Knowing the peace could be shattered at any moment kept him on edge.

Chapter Nineteen

Three days after their date, neither Kentley nor Clay had heard from Ryan Moss. The ranch relaxed despite the lingering sense of unease, and the boss's family returned home.

Breakfast was again a jovial time as they talked about their chores for the day and any antics of the day before. Kentley and Clay had decided on a supper picnic by the stream later that day. Something she looked forward to very much.

The question of where Ryan was and why he hadn't made another move plagued her, but she held on to the hope that maybe he had left Misty Hollow for reasons only he knew. Even the FBI were talking about heading back to Little Rock.

How long would Kentley keep looking over her shoulder before she could totally believe Ryan was gone?

The rest of the day passed like the one before and the one before that—working with Stormy, cleaning the barn—the routine chores kept her grounded in the here and now, instead of contemplating what might have happened if Ryan had stuck around. What made a madman turn away from his obsession?

Stormy gave her a playful bump as she cinched the saddle on the horse's back. Honey sat and watched with soulful eyes as if the horse might suddenly become dangerous and charge Kentley. Two of her favorite living beings stood right there beside her. The other she'd meet up with as soon as she finished in the barn.

Clay. The future held promise with Ryan gone. A future she looked forward to. One she never thought possible for a troublemaking foster child no one had wanted to adopt.

Saddle done, she led Stormy from the barn to where Clay waited near the paddock. "It's a beautiful evening for a picnic." She glanced at the cloudless sky.

"It is. No moon tonight, so we'll head back before dark. Mrs. White made fried chicken wraps and chocolate chip cookies. If I'm not mistaken, the thermos holds her famous lemonade." He grinned.

"Sounds yummy." She climbed into the saddle.

With Honey running up ahead, often veering off when she caught the scent of something, they headed into the trees. A squirrel chattered an objection as they disturbed it. A blue jay dove, warning them away.

Kentley laughed. The day couldn't be more perfect.

She kept her gaze on Clay's strong back. The way his muscles rippled through the tee-shirt he wore. How had she gotten so lucky to have such a wonderful man care for her the way he did?

A breeze kicked up, and she tugged her pink cowboy hat more firmly on her head, breathing deep of the forest scents of earth and pine. Dead leaves and pine needles muffled the thud of the horses' hooves. Occasionally, she heard the rustle of Honey running through the brush and wondered how anyone could be content to live in the noise and bustle of a city.

Clay cast a sexy smile over his shoulder, sending her heart skipping. "Getting hungry?"

"A little."

"We're almost there."

The sound of the stream burbling over rocks reached her ears before they broke through the trees. They let the horses free graze on a small patch of grass while Clay spread a threadbare quilt on the ground near the water.

Kentley removed the picnic basket from the back of his horse and carried it to the quilt. She toed off the boots that matched her hat, and set her hat next to her, shaking out her hair.

"You're always beautiful," Clay said, sitting beside her. "But, with the sun's rays filtering through the trees, setting your hair on fire, you more than beautiful."

She laughed. "That's impossible. You can't be more than something."

"Sure you can." He leaned over and kissed her. "Because you, darlin', most certainly are more than."

Heat rushed through her body, and she turned her attention to the picnic basket. Her embarrassment made Clay laugh harder.

"You need to learn to take a compliment."

She shrugged. "I'm not used to receiving them." She handed him a wrap and poured from the thermos into two cups. It was, indeed, lemonade. "It's nice to go out without an escort."

"Yep." Clay found a flat surface on the ground to set his cup. "Took some convincing to keep Willy and Levi from following us."

"Hmm." She bit into her wrap and watched Honey stare at something in the water. She wasn't sure they should've let down their guard. Ryan could still be out there, had to be somewhere close. Maybe he had something to do and would return. No one was expecting him to come back after almost three weeks of silence. She wasn't as trusting.

It wasn't long until she knew why that feeling wouldn't leave.

Ryan stepped from the shadows and aimed a gun at Clay.

Clay reached for his.

"Don't even think about it," Ryan said. "Kentley hasn't fulfilled her destiny, so I really don't want to shoot her, but I will. On your feet, cowboy. You and the dog are coming with me. Kentley, grab his gun and throw both yours and his in the creek."

"You've been lying in wait." How did he know she had a gun? Kentley lifted his from his belt in the back and hers from her back pocket, and tossed the guns into the water.

Ryan nodded. "Waiting for you two to think I'd gone. Looks like it worked."

She folded her hands in front of her to keep them from trembling. "Now what?"

"Cowboy will stay right here, and not call anyone. I'll text you our location with the time limit allowed for you to save him and your dog. Find something to tie around the dog's collar and tell her to behave. I don't need her in order to get you to do what I want." He narrowed his eyes. "I won't hesitate to shoot her."

~

He'd been a fool to think Moss had left Misty

Hollow. In his defense, he'd never dealt with a madman before. Now, he found himself with his hands tied behind his back being marched away from the woman Ryan wanted to kill.

"Where are you taking me?" He glanced down at Honey whose rope had been tied to Clay's belt. Growls emerged from the dog's throat. "Shhh, girl. We'll be okay." He knew without a doubt that Kentley would come for them. That was the plan after all.

"I've got a place, don't worry. A nice little vacant farmhouse in the middle of nowhere. I'll give Kentley plenty of time to come for you."

Clay's hands curled into fists. If he found the way to get free, he'd take Moss out before Kentley arrived. No way would he let the man go through with his diabolical mission.

The ranch would be on alert when they didn't return by dark. He could only pray that wouldn't be too late for them to track his phone. If Clay didn't find a way to free himself, he'd have to hold on until help came—before Moss took Kentley into the flames.

Moss led him to a rusty Ford truck and ushered him and the dog into the front seat. "Don't try anything to make me shoot you or the dog."

"The dog's name is Honey."

"Nothing sweet about her. She wants to bite my face off." Moss set his gun in his lap and turned the key in the ignition. A few minutes later they bounced down what could barely be called a road.

A ramshackle house appeared in the middle of a long-forgotten field. How in the world had the man found this place? Not a hunting cabin. Once a family might have lived there. Now the only residents would be mice and field critters.

Moss parked behind the house and ordered Clay from the truck. He pulled a cell phone from the glove compartment and sent a text. Most likely to Kentley.

"How long are you giving her to find us?"

"Two hours. Plenty of time for a woman on a mission. I've given her the coordinates to this place."

"What if she doesn't know how to follow them?"

He shrugged. "Then, I guess I'll have to come up with another plan to purge her because you'll be dead."

His heart sank at how callously the man spoke about Clay's death. As if Clay's life held no worth other than luring Kentley to her death. Terrified of fire or not, she would come. That's who she was.

She'd shove aside what terrified her the most and put her life in danger for him.

Moss poked Clay in the back with his pistol. "Move to the house."

Clay jerked around. "Stop doing that."

The other man laughed. "You want to kill me, don't you?"

"I will, given the chance."

"I doubt you'll get that chance, but we'll see. Now move."

Clay stepped into a house Moss had clearly been staying in. Footprints marred the thick dust on the floor. A sleeping bag had been spread across a sagging sofa. Canned food sat stacked on a rickety wooden table.

"Sorry to hear you plan on burning your house down."

"Shut up. Sit against that wall by the woodstove."

"You're going to burn me with that?"

"Lucky for you, the thing doesn't work." He used

the rope on Honey's collar to tie them both to the stove.

The dog snapped at him, causing Moss to jump backward. "Calm her down."

"Honey isn't my dog. She won't listen to me." Clay whispered, "Good girl."

Ryan made a noise in his throat and sat on the sofa. "When are you going to start the fire?"

"In a bit. Don't want the place flaming too early." He motioned his head toward a gas can. "Don't worry. I know what I'm doing. Everything will be timed perfectly."

That's what scared Clay. The man would make sure the house was engulfed when Kentley arrived or at least almost. He'd hide somewhere and watch her free Clay and Honey before making him stay inside with him while Clay watched from outside.

His gut clenched at the thought, stealing his breath as pain of what could happen ripped through him. He doubled over and ignored the taunting of Moss at what he considered weakness in a cowboy.

"Not so strong now, are you?" Moss sneered. "If Kentley comes for you, you'll live, so what are you afraid of? Oh, I know. You think you're in love with her."

"I know I am." He raised his head and glared, working the rope against the stove.

"Well, that's too bad. You've known all along that she belongs to me. That the two of us share a destiny."

"That only exists in your deluded mind."

Moss lunged to his feet and hit Clay across the face with the gun, slamming his head against the wall.

Honey leaped forward as much as the rope would allow, snarling and trying to clamp down on the man's arm.

Moss yelped and jumped back. "That was too close."

"Then I suggest you stay back," Clay said, spitting blood.

Moss paced the living room, occasionally stopping at the glassless window to stare out. The sun had started to set leaving them in a semi-darkness. "The fire will light this place up like daytime," he said. "Soon, very soon, I'll get things ready."

"I can hardly wait." Clay worked his hands faster until the man turned around, then he resumed his cowed expression, hoping he looked like a man accepting his fate rather than one fighting to survive.

He needed the man to leave. Maybe then, he could get Honey to chew through the rope.

Moss turned from the window. "It's time. Maybe I'll see you later." He took the gas can and left the house.

"Honey."

The dog turned her big head toward him.

"Chew." Clay glanced at the foot of rope between them. "Chew, girl."

She whined and licked his face.

"As much as I like your kisses, I need your help." He glanced at the rope again. "Come on, girl. Chew through. Please. I can't do this alone." His wrists burned from his efforts to free them. "We have to help Kentley."

The dog lowered her head and started to chew as the first flames licked the windowsill.

Chapter Twenty

Even with teeth as large as Honey's, getting through the rope took way too long. Clay coughed, keeping his nose and mouth as close to his chest as possible. An ache formed in his shoulders from his hunched position.

How much time had passed? Were they nearing the two-hour mark? Where was Moss?

His wrists grew sticky with perspiration and blood.

Honey whined as she gnawed on the rope, no doubt due to the fiberglass fibers hurting her mouth. Clay would make it up to her with a big, juicy steak once they were home safe.

Moss, a bandana over his nose and mouth, stepped into the house. He narrowed his eyes against the smoke. "Time is running out, my friend."

"I'm not your friend."

"The dog won't chew through in time. Don't you think I thought of that?" He clicked his tongue and shook his head. "You must think be thickheaded. That was a big mistake." The man glanced at his watch and returned outside.

Clay eyed the window. The flames seemed to be staying in that one area. Until Kentley arrived at least.

Then what? An explosion? Something that would cause the flames to spread faster?

A slight slip of the rope around his wrists sent hope springing upward. "Come on, girl. You're doing great."

When the rope slid from his wrist, he almost shouted with glee. Instead, he grabbed the chewed rope and led Honey to the back of the house where they climbed out a window. They got maybe a hundred yards away from the house before an explosion shook the ground.

Kentley hadn't arrived in time. He'd come so close to dying. Soon, shouts of outrage and cursing filled the air. Moss had discovered them missing.

Clay whipped around and sprinted into the brush, needing to reach Kentley before Moss did.

~

Ryan cursed and threw a rock into the flames. Once the small explosion caused the inferno to burn faster and hotter, he'd glanced through the open window hoping to see stark terror on the cowboy's face. Instead, he'd seen nothing.

The dog had succeeded in chewing through the rope. Now, they were headed back to warn Kentley. Ryan had to stop them.

His plan was ruined. He wouldn't be able to purge Kentley before taking her into eternity with him.

He cursed again and kicked the empty gas can. He didn't have any accelerant left over to pour over himself and Kentley. They'd have to die by bullets, something not nearly as grand or worthy enough to send them into the ever after.

This was the stupid cowboy's fault. Ryan would shoot the man on sight. He had no further use for him.

The dog, either.

With them gone, there would be nothing tethering Kentley to this world. He drew a sharp breath through his nose and stepped away from the fire in hopes of hearing someone coming through the trees.

Kentley might be late, but she didn't know the cowboy was gone. She'd still come. If she didn't arrive soon, he'd set off in search of her.

It would take a while for the cowboy to meet up with her. Neither of them knew where the other was. All hope was not lost for Ryan yet.

Things hadn't gone as he'd planned, but he was resourceful, adaptable. He touched the scars on his face. Was it really that important that Kentley be as scarred as he was? Maybe it was better that she entered eternity with her beauty intact. She didn't need to prove her heroism. Kentley had done so every time she'd gone to fight the fires that filled her with dread.

Yes. Things would be fine after all.

He waited another fifteen minutes, then sprinted in the direction the cowboy and dog had gone. He had a big surprise in mind. Huge.

~

Oh, no. Kentley pulled back on Stormy's reins. She was too late.

Tears poured down her cheeks. She'd lost Clay and Honey.

Not knowing how to read coordinates, she'd wasted time finding a spot where she had service on her cell phone, then she had to research how to read coordinates. It had wasted precious time Clay and Honey didn't have.

She slid from the horse's back and fell to the forest

floor. What would she do now? She'd lost everything important to her. Gone at the hands of a psycho.

The need to know the truth gave her the strength to go on. The forest had grown too dense for Stormy, so she left her. The horse could find her way home.

Kentley slung the backpack she'd stowed behind her saddle over one shoulder, swiped away her tears on the back of her hand, and then set off either to retrieve Clay's body, rescue him and Honey, or see that Ryan faced justice.

How remained a mystery. She had no idea where she was. Her only plan was to follow the smoke billowing in the distance, rising above the trees like silver thread against the night sky.

She jumped back and yelped, then hunkered down behind a massive pine tree trunk as something crashed through the bushes. Honey barged into sight. A second later, Clay joined her, soot smeared across his face.

"You aren't dead." Kentley threw herself into his arms.

He cupped her face. "Not yet." He kissed her. "We can't stay here. Moss will be coming for us."

"Do you know the way home?" She locked her gaze with his.

"Uh, maybe. I'm relying on Honey. She helped me find you." He patted the dog on the head. "If I hadn't been able to get her to understand that I needed her to chew through the rope, we'd have perished."

"She's pretty special." Kentley bent down and hugged her dog. "Let's go home."

"That sounds wonderful. We'll let the authorities know where Moss was last seen. Do you still have my phone?"

"Yes, but no service."

"They can still track it. Keep it turned on." He led the way down the path she'd been following for a few minutes, then veered off. "Moss can follow too easily if we stay on the path."

"You're bleeding." Kentley reached for his hand.

"I'll be fine." He coughed, then ordered Honey to lead them home. "Do you think she can?"

"If she follows the path I took, then yes." Kentley glanced behind them, expecting to see Ryan emerge from the shadows. She had no doubt he'd be coming for them. "We need to move faster."

The back of her neck prickled. Her shoulders tensed, expecting a bullet. Ryan would never let her out of the forest alive. Not now that his bait had escaped.

Once again, they didn't know where he was. The man was as elusive as a spark rising upward and just as dangerous. One spark could start a forest fire…she gasped. What if he set the woods on fire? They hadn't had rain in weeks. All he'd have to do was strike a match. She voiced her concern to Clay.

"I've thought of that myself. It's imperative we get out of here before that happens."

"We don't know where he is." She sped up to walk beside him. "He could set a fire in front of us."

"Then, we'll turn in another direction." He gave her hand a squeeze. "Dylan will be looking for us. All we have to do is hang on long enough to be found."

She wished she shared his optimism. She should. They were all still alive. Clay and Honey had escaped and found her. Why couldn't she believe they'd be rescued before Moss located them?

"Are we headed for the creek?" She thought she

heard it gurgling over the rocks.

"We may need to jump in it if he starts a forest fire. Plus, if we find the creek, I know how to get us home."

"There it is." Clay stopped and pointed at an orange glow. "Looks like it started at the cabin. All Moss has to do is set another one and force us to go in the direction he wants."

Fear clogged her throat. "He'll box us in."

"He'll try." Clay raced forward, holding low-hanging branches out of her way.

Honey glanced behind them and whined.

Something large crashed through the trees, then Stormy burst into view.

"Whoa." Clay grabbed the reins.

"We can ride out of here," Kentley said, putting one foot in the stirrup.

"Let's go." He swung up after her. With a flick of the reins, he sent the frightened horse toward the creek.

If they had to hide in the water, Stormy wouldn't have a chance. The creek wasn't deep enough for a horse to submerge itself. "We need to let Stormy go."

"We will once we reach the creek. There's a clearing there where we can be seen from the air. Plus, the trail from the ranch gives easy access. She'll know her way home from there."

Kentley hoped so.

A breeze picked up, moving the fire behind them faster. Another had started to their right. By the time they reached the creek, Kentley was shaking so much she thought she'd fall.

"Take a minute, sweetheart." Clay helped her sit on the quilt she'd left. "Looks like my horse has gone home. Since Moss hasn't cut us off, we can ride Stormy the rest of the way."

He reached for the horse's bridle. She nickered and tossed her head, then spun and galloped down the trail.

Kentley stared behind them. She could hear the crackle of the flames, smell the smoke. They didn't have a lot of time. She lunged to her feet. "Time to run."

Clay gripped her hand as they raced after the horse, his palm sticky from drying blood.

Another fire seemed to pop up on their left. They'd have to get close to the flames in order to continue down the path.

Moss stepped in front of them, a gun in his hand. "Looks like we'll all get purged after all."

"Are you crazy?" Clay lunged for him. "You've started multiple forest fires. It'll spread across this mountain in no time."

Moss fired at his feet. "The next bullet will be in your chest."

"You want us to just stand here and let the fire come?" Kentley glanced from Clay to Ryan.

"That's exactly what I want. This would already be over if the cowboy hadn't escaped. He and the—" He whipped around as Honey raced into the trees. "He'd be free to return to the ranch if you'd arrived at the house in time."

"Well, I didn't." Kentley's throat clogged. "I couldn't find my way. I'm not familiar with this mountain or following coordinates. Especially in the dark. Stop this, Ryan. Let us go."

"Not a chance." He kept the gun trained on them.

Honey leaped on him from behind.

The gun went off.

Kentley screamed and crumpled to the ground, her legs refusing to cooperate.

Clay fought Ryan for the gun, finally succeeding in taking it away from him when he dropped it because of the pressure Honey applied to his arm. He doubled up his fist and landed a right upper cut against the man's jaw.

Ryan fell unconscious to the ground as the thumping of a helicopter sounded overhead.

Kentley wrapped her arms around her middle, feeling to see how badly she was injured. She hissed when her fingers came into contact with the bullet's graze. She'd live, although the graze burned like someone had held a match to her skin.

"Are you all right?" Clay knelt beside her.

"I'm good. Secure Ryan." She glanced up between the tree branches. "Help has arrived."

"Let me see." He lifted up her shirt. "Just a graze." He leaned his forehead against hers. "When I saw you go down…"

"I know." She cupped his cheek. "I felt the same when I heard the explosion."

Willy and Levi raced toward them. "Let's get you guys out of here. The helicopter is about to start dropping water and Phos-Chek. We don't want to be here," Willy said.

Levi helped pull Kentley to her feet. "I caught Stormy and brought Clay's horse. You'll have rides back to the ranch. Go on. Willy and me will get Moss."

The two of them, followed by Honey, rushed to the waiting horses and the clear air of the meadow. Already, firemen and ranch hands beat at the flames to keep them from entering the pasture where the cows grazed.

Kentley prayed they could contain the fire to the few acres they'd sped through. Clay helped her onto Stormy's back. With one last glance at the burning woods, she turned the horse toward home.

Epilogue

Two weeks later, Kentley sat on the back deck, cup of coffee in hand while she waited for Clay. He'd told her at breakfast that he had a surprise for her.

With the danger of Moss behind them, work on the ranch had returned to normal. The twins were back in school, the diner almost rebuilt, and by spring, the forest should start to recover.

The fire chief said only ten acres had burned. Moss had known what he was doing, strategically placing the fires to box Clay and Kentley in. They'd been lucky.

The house he'd set on fire had burned completely to the ground and most of the land it had set on. Kentley had gone into the woods the other night, past the part that hadn't burned and been saddened by the blackened trees closer to the creek.

"Ready?" Clay smiled up at her from the bottom of the deck.

"Sure." She set her cup on the patio table and skipped down the steps to him. "Where are we going?"

"To the barn." He took her hand, his fingers entwining with hers.

Curiosity rose. What could he possibly want to show her? She had Blaze, what she'd named the kitten

Ryan had left her. She needed to get back to working with a new colt Dylan had recently purchased. A beautiful ebony little boy that would someday father many more.

He led her to Stormy's stall. Tacked to the wall was a white envelope. "Open it."

"Okay." She pulled a sheet of paper from the envelope. "What is this?"

"A bill of sale." He grinned. "I bought Stormy for you. All you have to do now is let Dylan mate her with Midnight when he's old enough and let him have the foal. I got a really good deal on her with that stipulation."

Tears sprang to her eyes. "She's mine?"

"All yours. Every cowhand needs their own horse, darlin'. Everyone knows that." He leaned against the stall.

"Why would you buy her for me?" She had nothing to give him in return. A horse like Stormy wouldn't have been cheap.

"I thought maybe...she could be a wedding gift." He pulled a ring box from the pocket of his jeans. "Kentley Montgomery, will you marry me? I don't have a ranch yet. We'd have to live in one of the tiny houses—you, me, Honey, and Blaze—but nothing would make me happier than to change your name to Jenkins." He opened the box to reveal a ruby ring surrounded by diamonds.

Oh, my. "It's beautiful." Did she dare say yes? He wanted to marry her—freckle-faced, red-haired, Kentley? What if he changed his mind before the wedding? She'd be heartbroken.

Everything in her wanted to take a chance on love. Did

she dare? She tore her gaze away from the ring then peered into Clay's eyes. "Is this for real, or am I dreaming?"

"It's not a dream, darlin'." He took a step closer. "Please say yes." The hand holding the ring box shook.

Stormy nodded, her mane flowing into her eyes as if she agreed that Kentley should marry Clay. She put her ear to the horse's mouth. "Is that so? Well, all right, then."

Kentley turned back to Clay. "Stormy seems to think I should say yes."

"She's a smart horse." His grin widened. "Honey gave me permission this morning."

"Oh, really?" Kentley arched a brow, enjoying the game of teasing.

"Absolutely. She agrees wholeheartedly. Honey would tell you herself if she wasn't napping under the magnolia tree."

Kentley laughed, then held out her hand. "I'd be honored to be your wife."

The ring fit perfectly.

"I don't want a big wedding, Clay. Just a small one here on the ranch with the ranch hands in attendance. Is that okay?"

"Will you wear a dress?" He grinned and tilted his head.

"Yes." She stepped into his arms and peered up at him. "A white one with puff sleeves and lots of lace."

"Hideous, but even you could make something like that look beautiful."

~

A week later, as a sunrise of crimson and coral kissed the top of the mountain, Kentley, with Honey at her side, ambled down a rose petal-strewn path that ran against the paddock where Stormy looked on.

Kentley wore a simple white silk dress with an uneven hem that skimmed her knees, white cowboy boots, and a white cowboy hat with a small veil attached to the front. Honey carried a smaller version of the white daisy bouquet in her mouth.

Kentley had never felt more beautiful in her entire life. The sheen of moisture in Clay's eyes when his gaze landed on her had her walking on air. That handsome man was all hers.

She took her place in front of him and set her bouquet on a small table near an arch adorned with fairy lights and white sheeting. Smiling, she placed her hands in those off her husband-to-be.

"Truly beautiful," he whispered. "So much better than the dress you described."

A giggle escaped her. "I changed my mind." She'd had no intention of wearing anything remotely like the dress she'd described when he'd proposed. Simplicity worked best on this red-haired cowgirl.

Clay's hands tightened on hers as the pastor started to speak. "Dearly beloved…"

She realized she'd missed most of what the pastor said when she heard the words, "I now pronounce you husband and wife."

Every dream for her future—dreams of a husband and a home of her own—came true when the pastor told Clay he could kiss his bride.

He lowered his head and claimed her lips in a kiss so sweet she grinned through her tears when he pulled away.

The End

Dear Reader,

I hope you enjoyed this story about a foster girl who wanted a family. There are many people in the world who don't feel worthy of love. Let's help them when we see them.

If you enjoyed Kentley's story, please leave a review. Reviews are very important to an author and help Amazon's algorithms show the book to more people.

God Bless,

Cynthia

www.cynthiahickey.com

Cynthia Hickey is a multi-published and best-selling author of cozy mysteries and romantic suspense. She has taught writing at many conferences and small writing retreats. She and her husband run the publishing press, Winged Publications. They live in Arizona and Arkansas, becoming snowbirds with three dogs. They have ten grandchildren who keep them busy and tell everyone they know that "Nana is a writer."

Connect with me on FaceBook
Twitter
Sign up for my newsletter and receive a free short story
www.cynthiahickey.com

Follow me on Amazon
And Bookbub
Shop my bookstore on shopify. For better price and autographed books. You can also subscribe to Mysterious Delivery, a mystery and suspense monthly book subscription with a book and several surprise goodies to pamper the reader.

Enjoy other books by Cynthia Hickey

Cowboys of Misty Hollow
Cowboy Jeopardy
Cowboy Peril
Cowboy Hazard
Cowgirl Blaze

Misty Hollow
Secrets of Misty Hollow
Deceptive Peace
Calm Surface
Lightning Never Strikes Twice
Lethal Inheritance
Bitter Isolation
Say I Don't
Christmas Stalker
Bridge to Safety
When Night Falls
A Place to Hide
Mountain Refuge

Stay in Misty Hollow for a while. Get the entire series here!

The Seven Deadly Sins series
Deadly Pride
Deadly Covet
Deadly Lust
Deadly Glutton
Deadly Envy
Deadly Sloth

Deadly Anger

The Tail Waggin' Mysteries
Cat-Eyed Witness
The Dog Who Found a Body
Troublesome Twosome
Four-Legged Suspect
Unwanted Christmas Guest
Wedding Day Cat Burglar

Brothers Steele
Sharp as Steele
Carved in Steele
Forged in Steele
Brothers Steele (All three in one)

The Brothers of Copper Pass
Wyatt's Warrant
Dirk's Defense
Stetson's Secret
Houston's Hope
Dallas's Dare
Seth's Sacrifice
Malcolm's Misunderstanding
The Brothers of Copper Pass Boxed Set

Time Travel
The Portal

Tiny House Mysteries
No Small Caper
Caper Goes Missing
Caper Finds a Clue
Caper's Dark Adventure
A Strange Game for Caper
Caper Steals Christmas
Caper Finds a Treasure
Tiny House Mysteries boxed set

Wife for Hire – Private Investigators
Saving Sarah
Lesson for Lacey
Mission for Meghan
Long Way for Lainie
Aimed at Amy
Wife for Hire (all five in one)

A Hollywood Murder
Killer Pose, book 1
Killer Snapshot, book 2
Shoot to Kill, book 3
Kodak Kill Shot, book 4
To Snap a Killer
Hollywood Murder Mysteries

Shady Acres Mysteries
Beware the Orchids, book 1
Path to Nowhere
Poison Foliage

Poinsettia Madness
Deadly Greenhouse Gases
Vine Entrapment
Shady Acres Boxed Set

CLEAN BUT GRITTY Romantic Suspense

Highland Springs

Murder Live
Say Bye to Mommy
To Breathe Again
Highland Springs Murders (all 3 in one)

Colors of Evil Series

Shades of Crimson
Coral Shadows

The Pretty Must Die Series

Ripped in Red, book 1
Pierced in Pink, book 2
Wounded in White, book 3
Worthy, The Complete Story

Lisa Paxton Mystery Series

Eenie Meenie Miny Mo
Jack Be Nimble

Hickory Dickory Dock
Boxed Set

Hearts of Courage
A Heart of Valor
The Game
Suspicious Minds
After the Storm
Local Betrayal
Hearts of Courage Boxed Set

Overcoming Evil series
Mistaken Assassin
Captured Innocence
Mountain of Fear
Exposure at Sea
A Secret to Die for
Collision Course
Romantic Suspense of 5 books in 1

INSPIRATIONAL

Nosy Neighbor Series
Anything For A Mystery, Book 1
A Killer Plot, Book 2
Skin Care Can Be Murder, Book 3
Death By Baking, Book 4
Jogging Is Bad For Your Health, Book 5
Poison Bubbles, Book 6

A Good Party Can Kill You, Book 7
Nosy Neighbor collection

Christmas with Stormi Nelson

The Summer Meadows Series
Fudge-Laced Felonies, Book 1
Candy-Coated Secrets, Book 2
Chocolate-Covered Crime, Book 3
Maui Macadamia Madness, Book 4
All four novels in one collection

The River Valley Mystery Series
Deadly Neighbors, Book 1
Advance Notice, Book 2
The Librarian's Last Chapter, Book 3
All three novels in one collection

Historical cozy
Hazel's Quest

Historical Romances
Runaway Sue
Taming the Sheriff
Sweet Apple Blossom
A Doctor's Agreement
A Lady Maid's Honor
A Touch of Sugar

Love Over Par
Heart of the Emerald
A Sketch of Gold
Her Lonely Heart

Finding Love the Harvey Girl Way
Cooking With Love
Guiding With Love
Serving With Love
Warring With Love
All 4 in 1

Finding Love in Disaster
The Rancher's Dilemma
The Teacher's Rescue
The Soldier's Redemption

Woman of courage Series

A Love For Delicious
Ruth's Redemption
Charity's Gold Rush
Mountain Redemption
They Call Her Mrs. Sheriff
Woman of Courage series

Short Story Westerns
Flowers of the Desert

Contemporary

Romance in Paradise
Maui Magic
Sunset Kisses
Deep Sea Love
3 in 1

Finding a Way Home
Service of Love
Hillbilly Cinderella
Unraveling Love
I'd Rather Kiss My Horse

Christmas
Dear Jillian
Romancing the Fabulous Cooper Brothers
Handcarved Christmas
The Payback Bride
Curtain Calls and Christmas Wishes
Christmas Gold
A Christmas Stamp
Snowflake Kisses
Merry's Secret Santa
A Christmas Deception

The Red Hat's Club (Contemporary novellas)

Finally
Suddenly

Surprisingly
The Red Hat's Club 3 – in 1

Short Story

One Hour (A short story thriller)
Whisper Sweet Nothings (a Valentine short romance)

www.ingramcontent.com/pod-product-compliance
Lightning Source LLC
Chambersburg PA
CBHW070423310726
48977CB00003B/815